Destination Unexpected

Destination Unexpected

short stories edited by
Donald R. Gallo

CANDLEWICK PRESS
CAMBRIDGE, MASSACHUSETTS

Library of Congress Cataloging-in-Publication Data

Destination unexpected : short stories / edited by Donald R. Gallo. — 1st ed.
p. cm.
Contents: Something old, something new / by Joyce Sweeney — Brutal interlude /
by Ron Koertge — Bread on the water / by David Lubar — My people / by Margaret
Peterson Haddix — Bad blood / by Will Weaver — Keep smiling / by Alex Flinn —
August lights / by Kimberly Willis Holt — The kiss in the carryon bag / by Richard
Peck — Mosquito / by Graham Salisbury — Tourist trapped / by Ellen Wittlinger.
ISBN 0-7636-1764-4
1. Young adult fiction, American. [1. Coming of age — Fiction.
2. Short stories.] I. Gallo, Donald R.
PZ5.D47 2003
[Fic] — dc21   2002071599

2 4 6 8 10 9 7 5 3 1

Printed in the United States of America

This book was typeset in Garamond.

Candlewick Press
2067 Massachusetts Avenue
Cambridge, Massachusetts 02140

visit us at www.candlewick.com

This one is for worldwide travelers Chris and Dave.

D. R. G.

Introduction

Stories about journeys have interested listeners since the beginning of language. Literary history is filled with stories in which the main character goes on a journey that leads not only to a predetermined goal but also to the character's self-understanding. Arriving at the destination is the goal, certainly, but the experiences during the journey itself are what transform the character. In addition, the most important experiences are often those not expected. In classical literature, think of Odysseus's adventures after the Trojan War, Moses and the Israelites wandering in the wilderness, Huckleberry Finn on the raft floating down the Mississippi River.

In contemporary novels for teens, many journeys, such as Jason's in *Jason's Gold* by Will Hobbs, involve physical survival. Other journeys are mainly emotional and intellectual, as occurs in *Mind's Eye* by Paul Fleischman. Most journey stories, however, are a combination of those: Joan Bauer's *Rules of the Road*, Richard Peck's *A Long Way from Chicago*, Carolyn Coman's *Many Stones*. What's important is what the characters learn about themselves and others along the way.

The journey need not be long, nor the destination exotic. It can be as simple as a walk around the block where you see something you never noticed before. In David Lubar's story, "Bread on the Water," Tommy's insights come after a short walk to the local diner just down the street. For Darius, in Joyce Sweeney's "Something Old, Something New," revelation comes on a bus ride across town into neighborhoods where he's never been before. Helene, in Ellen Wittlinger's "Tourist Trapped," travels much farther, leaving her home in Kansas one summer to find something very different from what she expected on Cape Cod. But for Mick, in Kimberly Willis Holt's "August Lights," it's just a short walk on the golf course outside his family's Texas home. These and six other characters discover surprising things about their worlds and, more importantly, about themselves in these ten stories about journeys.

No matter how long or short the journey, it must begin, as the Chinese proverb says, with a single step. So, step into this collection of stories by award-winning authors and travel along with these teenage characters. One will take you to Cape Cod, as I said; one to rural Ohio; another to the highlands of Hawaii. You can ride with Samantha in a pickup truck to summer camp, stay with Lindley at a college program for gifted students, visit a horseracing track with Lori and Lincoln, or meet royalty in a European country. Take your time; there's no rush. And if you find your fictional companion uninteresting or not to your liking in one story, pick a different traveler elsewhere in the book. Enjoy your journey. Perhaps you'll even learn something about yourself along the way.

Don Gallo

Success is not a place at which one arrives but rather . . . the spirit with which one undertakes and continues the journey.

— Alex Noble
"In Touch with the Present"
Christian Science Monitor, March 1979

So every journey that I make
Leads me . . .
To some new ambush, to some fresh mistake . . .

— Philip Larkin (1922–1986)
"Nursery Tale"

A bus ride across town doesn't mean much to most people,
but for Darius, a young writer, it's a journey
into a totally different world.

Something Old, Something New

Joyce Sweeney

Here I am, Lord of the Geeks, broiling in the afternoon
sun, wearing an outfit so strange, some guy just swerved
his bike right in front of a car so he could get a better look.

I'll describe my outfit so you can laugh, too. I'm
wearing my brother David's khaki pants from the Gulf
War (I try not to picture chemical and biological agents
surrounding my Boys), an old pink dress shirt of my
dad's that my mom couldn't bear to throw away, a blue
corduroy blazer Aunt Ginny found at the Salvation Army
store, and a red clip-on bow tie my little brother Neb
got me at the Dollar Store. Everyone was trying to help,

getting me presentable for this big moment in the life of Darius Holmsby. I'm wearing something old, something new, something borrowed, and something blue.

Did I mention the heat? I decide to shuck the jacket, so I don't show up at the "gala" as one giant pit stain. Dad's pink shirt flares in the Florida sun. The other people going to this gala are taking their afternoon naps in Whiteland, not needing to shower and dress until six, when they'll slide into their air-conditioned Lexuses and BMWs and drive on over to the Coral Springs Library (I picture something like the Taj Mahal) to see the Boy from Section Eight housing who won their short story contest.

I know what you're thinking. But they didn't pick me for PR reasons. It was what they call a blind judging, meaning they picked the story first and then saw it was written by Darius Holmsby from Euclid Avenue, where all of them pray their cars never break down. They still don't know I'm a kid. I talked to a lady on the phone, but I have a real deep voice for sixteen, and I could tell by the way she kept calling me Mr. Holmsby, she thought I was grown.

So here's my itinerary for this afternoon—if it ever comes before I have a heat stroke: I catch the 61 South bus and take it all the way to the downtown terminal. Elapsed time, sixty minutes. At the terminal, I have a twenty-minute wait because of how the connection is. Then I catch the number 2 North, which will drive me for forty minutes back the way I came, only angling westward into the magical land of Coral Springs, a place I've never been, but I know what it is. Every house has a pool, every mom has an SUV, all the kids play soccer and practice for the SATs. I'm scared about this part of the trip. Will there be anyone black on the bus? Should I sit in the back and be invisible or plop down in front to show I don't care? Rosa Parks, I'm not.

But wait, there's more. Because Coral Springs has three different buses to serve its twenty-block area, I still have to transfer again, this time at the Coral Square Mall, to the 83 bus, which will get me to the Taj Mahal at the stroke of seven. The Coral Square Mall. I see the whole cast of 90210 gliding past the bus stop, talking on their cell phones, maybe dropping a quarter in my lap so I can get a good hot meal. A surge of sweaty adrenaline hits me so hard I almost turn and run back up my walk, but I think of Neb buying me this stupid tie and I know Mom and Aunt Ginny are watching me out the window, so I square up my shoulders. I can always bail downtown.

The 61 rounds the corner, belching and coughing, and opens its hissing jaws. I buy an all-day student pass with the picture of the smiling bee, ignore the stare the driver gives my glowing shirt, and sit down. Everyone else on the bus is African-American and female. They look bone tired. Every one of them turns her face away from me and I realize it's because with this lame jacket and tie, they think I'm a religious fanatic.

◦ ◦ ◦

Maybe you think I hate white people. I don't. I don't know enough of them to have an opinion. Which makes me scared of them but that's not the same as hate, even though I know the two can look alike.

But to balance all this "fear" you're hearing, I'll tell you that one of my favorite people in the world is white—my English teacher, Mr. Gould. Mr. Gould takes being white to the extreme: he's so pale you can see all his thoughts and feelings erupting in little blushes and flushes under his skin. The kids call him Mr. Ghoul, but that doesn't mean they don't like him. It's just that you have to call a teacher something. There's a handful of white teachers at our school, but the rest of them are scared of us and keep their arms down at their sides when they walk the halls.

Mr. Gould reaches out, literally. When we handed in our first essay back in October, he asked to see me after class. I figured he was going to accuse me of plagiarism— I get that a lot—but he just handed me my paper and said, "Darius, you're gifted." When he said the word "gifted," his hand came out and the fingers touched my shoulder, like a brand. Or like the Queen when she makes knights. *I dub you Sir Gifted.* His little tap knocked the wind out of me. I couldn't speak.

He frowned at my stunned expression and said, "What? I'm the first person who ever told you that? Are you kidding?"

He was the one who found this contest, sponsored by the Florida Center for the Book. "Let's see how well you can do, Darius, in a contest where nobody knows who you are or where you live. Where it's just your writing out there alone. You'll be competing with adults, maybe even professional writers. Even if you got an honorable mention, think what that would tell you."

It has told me. When I got First Place, it told me my dream of being a Real Writer wasn't just a stupid idea in my head. Getting the prize was enough, but when I told Mr. Gould I wasn't going to the "gala" to get my award, he shook his head like it wasn't an option. "If you're afraid to go claim what's yours, Darius, you'll never make it. The writing world is too competitive. You have the talent, but you need courage, too. You have to be a warrior. This is a good place to start. You can do this."

Lucky me. Mr. Gould had to have his wedding anniversary tonight, and for some crazy reason he picked his wife over me, sending me into this war zone by myself. But I carry his words. *Talent* and *courage*.

My father had talent. My brother David had courage. They're both in jail. Maybe the trick is to learn to put the two things together.

A crazy man gets on the bus. "Hey, hey, hey," he says to the driver, making Quaalude gestures with his hands—a big octopus waving his tentacles. He drops some change in the box and waits for the verdict.

"You're thirty cents short," says the driver. You hear hope in his voice.

The crazy man turns into a snake and juts his head closer to the driver—he couldn't have heard right. "Whaaaaa?"

The rest of the passengers glance at him and away, like you do around a dangerous dog.

"Thirty cents." The driver gently pushes the guy out of his personal zone. "Let's go, man. I'm on a schedule."

Looking baffled, the crazy man turns to us, the jury. "Thirty cent?" he asks. His voice seems to float.

I have a ten and ten ones in my pocket. Aunt Ginny took it out of the grocery jar to give to me because she doesn't trust this whole contest and she's sure they're going to charge me admission or make me buy something and she doesn't want me embarrassed. It's not a lack of faith in me; it's a lack of faith in everyone else. I find myself standing up, digging out my wallet, calling to the driver. "I'll pay his fare."

All the women on the bus glare at me. Now we have to ride with the crazy man for however long. But I don't care. I walk up and put a dollar in the slot.

"Oh, thank you, son." The crazy man clamps onto my shoulder. "Bless you. God will bless you."

The driver refunds the crazy man's seventy cents to him.

"Here!"

I'm walking down the aisle to my seat, but he's right behind me, breathing on me. Instead of alcohol, he smells like ether, a new one on me. "Take this—take this." He wants to give me the seventy cents. His voice sounds dangerously close to tears.

"It's okay." I slide into my seat. "Keep it."

He sits across from me with his legs in the aisle. "Bless you, son. Jesus, He sees you and He will bless you."

I can feel the heat from all the angry stares on me. Including the driver, who now has to watch in that little mirror to make sure the crazy man behaves.

"Thanks," I mutter and stare hard out my window. We're going past a playground that has no grass. It's all asphalt. If a kid fell off the monkey bars, he'd bust his head open.

The crazy man begins to sing. " 'You'll never miss the water till the well runs dry . . .' "

I fight tears. God is not blessing me, He's mocking me. That was one of Dad's songs.

My father's favorite word was *class*. Everything in the world that was good had class. Everything that was bad had no class. When he was about my age, someone told him he was gifted in music. And his mother, Granny Lynn, took two jobs so he could take lessons: drums, piano, guitar, voice. Whatever he wanted. Like me, he won a prize at sixteen. There was a band contest down in Miami and his group, Sloe Gin Fizz, got to play a whole season at Disney World. That got his hopes up, which my mother said turned him into a permanent fool. She met him when he was twenty, playing a club in Miami. She was sent to audit the books, and she shut the place down, but Dad went out with her anyway. In those days he could always get jobs. What the owners liked was that he was versatile. He could sing like Eddie Grant or Earth, Wind and Fire. He could belt it out like James Brown or croon like Smokey or even strut and chirp like Prince. But his real passion was the ancient music like Duke Ellington or the Mills Brothers. The groundbreakers, he called them. They had class. And whenever he played a club, he would work in one old song like "Paper Doll" and it would always get raves. He worked a circuit of clubs all around Florida, and whenever he had the money, he'd buy a plane ticket to Vegas—the classiest city on Earth—and try to get the job that would "set us up."

At first my mom liked all this. It was a partnership. She was the practical one and Dad brought in all the adventure and glamour. She expected him to have a big break and then she'd be his manager. Dad was like an investment that would pay off someday.

This whole good part of their marriage was before I was born, when David was little. He even got to go on two trips with Daddy to Vegas and watch him audition.

He also said there was a lot of drinking—in the hotel room—before and after each verdict.

The part I remember was us never knowing what city he was in or when he'd be back, and Aunt Ginny moving in to help with the bills and, later, the baby. Now and then he'd show up and we'd all get hopeful, but then he'd ask Mom for money and they'd fight and he'd drink and sleep on the couch and after a few days he'd leave again. It wasn't very classy at all.

He wrote me a letter last year from the facility he's in in Nevada. He explained about his addictions and diseases and how he started gambling more and more and he borrowed money from some bad guys and then he had to break the law to pay them back. Since he used a weapon in the commission of a crime, he won't come up for parole for another fifteen years. People point out to me that I talk about him in the past tense, like he's dead. I never do that with David. I guess I still have hope for David.

We're at the terminal. The crazy man has been singing "Just My Imagination" for the last two minutes. We all get off except him.

"Come on," I hear the driver say behind me. "It's the end of the line."

Waiting at the terminal, I take out my award-winning short story and pretend to read it over because there's a white lady walking up to everyone and trying to talk to them. She's too far away for me to hear what it's about, but it's either everybody's salvation or she's short for bus fare and I already did my good deed for the day.

I hunch over the folded pages and read, " 'Caged' by Darius Holmsby." I wonder how many people entered the contest besides me and what they were like. The story is about my brother David and the day the cops came for him and we found out that the great office job he had was running numbers in Overtown. My Aunt Ginny turned on David and said there's nothing worse than a liar and if he had told us out in the open he was a criminal, it would have been better. Well, she's got a reason to hate liars with her man-history, but I understood David. He was a hero in the Gulf War, decorated three times. The army never cared if he was poor and lived in Section Eight housing. He wrote me a letter and said that in the army, *Section Eight* means crazy and we got a good laugh out of that. But the army loved David because he was strong and fast and smart. He had courage. His commander said he had the ability to override his emotions, which was the best thing a soldier could do. Even when he was scared, he would keep going forward, doing his mission, making the right thing happen. Then he got wounded and had to come home. He was a hero around the neighborhood for about one week and then he was just a guy on disability with stories nobody wanted to hear. He needed to keep the hero thing going and one way to do that around Euclid Avenue is to get a "good job" and bring money home. That was his new mission and he did it by whatever means necessary.

I think of David in prison. I have bad dreams about the stuff I saw when I went to visit him. In my dreams, they mistake me for David and lock me up.

"Hello?" The white lady is standing right over me.

I look up, squinting. It's five-thirty and the sun is at that low angle that can kill you. She's a little fat lady, with a turned-up nose, like a pig, maybe fifty years old. She says a jabber of things to me in French and tries to hand me a folded piece of notepaper. At least this doesn't seem to be about my salvation. I'm taking my second year of French in high school. It's pretty funny to hear all of us poor kids chanting in unison, "Waiter! Please return the veal. It is overcooked." I make straight A's in French, but I can't keep up with this woman's rapid-fire monologue, except that it's laced with "*s'il vous plaît*" and she's calling me Monsieur. Since it's too flat to be a bomb, I take the note and look at it.

Please help me! I do not speak English and I am
unfamiliar with the transit system of Fort Lauderdale.
I am traveling from Pompano Beach to the downtown
terminal, where I must transfer to the 54 West. I need
to get off the bus at the corner of Margate Blvd. and
State Road Seven, where my daughter will meet me.
Please help me if I am lost and get me to the right bus.

My nickname among my friends is Easy because I'm known for not showing my temper, but the note makes my blood pressure shoot up like a skyrocket. What crazy person would send this poor, defenseless woman out into the city with this "rob me, I'm vulnerable" note? Putting this lady in the downtown terminal is like throwing a bunny rabbit in an alligator pit, with a note pinned on him that says, "Please don't eat him, he's my pet." What's wrong with people?

She points to the note now. *"Anglais,"* she insists.

"Qui est-ce qui a écrit ceci?" I ask. *"Votre fille?"* I want to know whom to hate.

She clasps her hands with joy. *"Français! Vous parlez français, Monsieur!"*

Monsieur. That kills me. *"Un peu."* I pinch my fingers to show just how small the "peu" is. *"Qui est-ce qui a écrit ceci?"*

She tells me her brother wrote it. He has to go to a— something—and she can't live with him anymore. He was her rock. Now she has to live with her daughter. La, la, la. (This seems to mean living with her daughter will be no *pique-nique*.) Her daughter will meet her at the bus stop in Mar-get if she can only get there. Can I help her, please?

I get up, tell her yes, I can help her. She declares me an angel. I find the 54 bus idling, the driver having a Mountain Dew. He looks like a big, lanky, white cowboy with his hat tipped back.

"Hi," I begin.

He looks at me suspiciously, with my clown outfit and my white lady in tow.

"She can't speak English, but she needs to get on your bus and get off at Margate and State Road Seven." I show him the note.

He sits up and reads it, frowning. "This is irresponsible," he says. "Is she related to you?"

This seems like a silly question but I just say, "No, but I thought somebody ought to help her." Again, I find myself digging into my wallet, getting out Aunt Ginny's cynicism money. "Let me pay her fare."

The French lady screams several exclamations at this.

"That's nice of you, son. Don't worry. I'll treat her like my own grandma. What are people thinking, to send her out like that?"

"I don't know." I tell the lady in French that everything is taken care of; this man will tell her what to do next. She thanks me and thanks me, calls me an angel, her guardian angel, a saint, and a word I don't recognize. I walk away exhausted. And I'm still an hour and a half and two buses from my award.

The number 2 bus arrives at the terminal. It is a shiny new bus that doesn't cough and wheeze. Everyone lining up for it is white. Fear shoots through me, even though no one is paying any attention to me at all. I hang toward the back of the line, and then I think, *Why am I being all meek?* So I take a seat right in the front of the bus. Then I regret that because I feel vulnerable with my back to all of them. I think of the snipers my brother David told me about. Then I think how stupid all my feelings are. These people couldn't care less about me.

I look out the window and watch the landscape change, like some tourist seeing the Alaskan wilderness or something. The houses get bigger and bigger, with more and more grass and trees every block we go. No cars on blocks. No wash on lines. And people have bird feeders in their backyards. That's got to be the height of disposable income. When you have enough left over to put out food for animals that know how to take care of themselves.

An African-American woman gets on the bus. She wears a business suit and jewelry and has a briefcase that she rests in her lap. She catches me staring at her. Because my street is all black, I figured Coral Springs would be all white. When she gets off the bus, several teenage girls, also black, get on. I feel disoriented, like I've just been shown a flaw in the law of gravity.

My little brother Neb gave me this stupid tie last night. The poor little guy's given name is Nebuchadnezzar. He's six. We call him Lollipop at home, because he's so sweet.

All the female relatives talk about the damage he'll do to womanhood some day. He is also obsessed with money and has several piggy banks in his room. When he has to give a gift, he'll do something like draw around his hand and sign his name. So when he gave me a wrapped package last night, I could hardly believe it.

"What's this about, Neb?" I asked, tearing off the wrapping paper.

I took it out and looked at it. The ugliest, cheapest-looking tie I'd ever seen.

"I spent a whole dollar," he told me. "You need to look right for the library people because they'll have a tie on."

I gave him a hug. "You are the best brother in the whole world."

"Cut it out!" He squirmed away. "You'll squish me."

"I am. I'm going to squish you right now." And I chased him all around the room.

I love him, and I know he loves me, but there's more to it than that. His father and his other brother are in jail. I'm Neb's only hope.

Right now, the tie feels like some kind of *Silence of the Lambs* caterpillar trying to crawl up my throat. It's six-fifteen and the sky is orange and I'm sitting on a beautiful, varnished wooden bench at the dreaded Coral Square Mall. Even if my final bus is late, I will get to the Taj Mahal in time. I've been traveling for two hours and fifteen minutes now and I'm numb from my shoulders to my knees. The bee logo on my all-day pass looks pretty sad. But I was wrong about Coral Springs.

Oh, the cast of 90210 is here all right. I've never seen so many different kinds of cell phones walking around. But I see Hispanic people, Asian people, African-American people. And more than that, these are all regular people here. I see teenage mothers pushing strollers, evangelists, crazy men, lost women—everything I've seen everywhere else is here, too.

Now, a girl who is a cross between Tori Spelling and Ava Savalot sits down next to me on the bench. She is crying quietly into a tissue. Well, of course. I started the day playing Good Samaritan and my mocking friend, God, is going to keep it that way. I offer her my handkerchief, Mom's contribution to my ensemble. Where she even found a handkerchief in this day and age is beyond me, but I whip it out like Sir Galahad and say, "You okay?"

She looks at me. My outfit doesn't make her run for the hills. Maybe she takes me for some preppie computer geek who doesn't care for worldly things.

"This guy . . ." she begins and breaks down in loud weeping. Her nails are polished to look like pale pink pearls.

I know that story. Aunt Ginny tells it every Saturday night. "No guy is worth this," I say, stealing Mom's line.

"My mom warned me . . . and the worst part is, I have to call her for a ride home now because he left me here . . . the dirty . . ." She doesn't have a good word.

"Dog?" I suggest.

That makes her laugh. She's a nice girl. We're just a couple of nice teenagers sharing a laugh. I feel so free, almost like I could fly. "You could take the bus home," I suggest.

She blushes. "I don't know how. And anyway, I spent all my cash. All I have are my credit cards."

"Poor baby," I say. But I mean it as a joke and she takes it that way. This morning, I would have hated her.

I take out the cynicism money for the third time and hand her a dollar. I take out my Coral Springs bus schedules. "Tell me where you live and I'll tell you what to do."

It isn't the Taj Mahal, but it's not exactly what I'd call a library, either. The library in my neighborhood has dark, old wood with mouse chewings on it and a card catalog and a lot of drooling perverts. This thing is like Frasier Crane's apartment—all golden wood and sculptures sitting around and art on display. I walk up to an information desk as big as a nurse's station. My fear is all gone. Somehow the bus ride took it out of me. I feel like David in combat, going forward to make things right. "I'm Darius Holmsby," I say. "I won the short story contest."

The lady smiles. "The gala is back there in room C." She points to an open archway.

Okay, I have a little adrenaline surge as I walk down a blind corridor, hearing polite white laughter filtering out of the doorway I have to go in. But I go in. Everyone is dressed like movie stars. They are all ages, mostly white but not all. All look confident and secure. They hold glasses of wine and cheese cubes on little toothpicks. What the hell am I doing here? I just stand still and one by one they seem to notice me. The conversation and laughing wind down. They just stare at me in Aunt Ginny's thrift-shop jacket and Daddy's nightclub shirt and David's combat pants and Neb's hopeful tie. Something old. Something new.

"I'm Darius Holmsby," I say.

They react with shock but surge forward like pigeons on a bag of bread. They start introducing themselves, Mrs. Whatever with the library foundation and Mr. Something Else, the local author. No one can believe I'm sixteen. And no one cares. They want to tell me about my story, how much they liked it. Mr. Something Else compares me to Richard Wright. They mean it. My writing is all they care about. Somebody makes a joke about how I can't have a glass of wine and runs to get me a Coke. I just wish Aunt Ginny could see this.

"Is your story based on fact, Darius?" asks the lady who brings me the Coke and a little sandwich. Everyone waits for my answer.

"It's about my brother," I begin. I feel no fear. I'm a writer talking to writers. Mr. Gould is right. I can do this.

❋

ABOUT THE AUTHOR

Joyce Sweeney entered the field of books for teenagers by winning the first Delacorte Press Prize for an Outstanding First Young Adult Novel for *Center Line.* That novel and three of her other books—*Shadow, The Tiger Orchard,* and *The Spirit Window*—have been designated Best Books for Young Adults by the American Library Association, and her recent *Players* was among *Booklist*'s Top Ten Sports Books. A resident of Coral Springs, Florida, she writes about friendships, family relationships, and the serious concerns of contemporary teenagers, with self-discovery being a main outcome in most of her novels and stories.

Her short story about Darius's bus trip across town reflects her own association with city buses. Growing up in Dayton, Ohio, she rode buses everywhere because her family couldn't afford to buy a car. Then, at sixteen, at the same time she discovered she had a learning disability that prevented her from driving, she realized that she was the only kid in her crowd whose parents were not affluent. "But being a talented writer," she says, "seemed to equalize everything in my mind, made me feel like I could hold my head up, even as I was begging my friends for rides and ignoring their pitying comments about my use of mass transit. Somewhere in there you have Darius."

Joyce Sweeney's newest novel, *Headlock,* is a thriller about a group of kids, all fans of professional wrestling, who are held hostage by a desperate gunman who picked the wrong house to rob.

A trip to the racetrack helps Lori examine her relationship with her boyfriend, Lincoln. Is he a winner? Don't bet on it.

Brutal Interlude

Ron Koertge

Lincoln follows me in like he owns the place.

"Is your mom home, Lori?"

"Beats me," I say.

He cups both hands around his mouth. "Mrs. Armstrong." He makes my last name long and singsongy, like he's crooning for a lost hiker.

"Alone at last," he says, licking his chops like the Big Bad Wolf.

Then he goes right to the refrigerator. Our refrigerator. He paws through it, grabs a little plate with a wedge of cheese on it, and carries that into the TV room. He looks funny holding it, funny eating it. Chomping away. I'm wondering if that was going to be our dinner. Mine and Mom's. With some grapes and pita bread. A glass of wine for her, iced tea for me. Too late now.

Lincoln wipes his fingers on his shirt and reaches for the remote. On comes MTV. Gyrating girls. A band even I've heard of. Lincoln plays air guitar. Lying down. Supine. But I don't use that word, a word he doesn't know.

I concentrate on his shoes. They're huge. Big as badgers. Did I never notice that before?

"When I get my band going," he says, "you can book gigs for us."

"Right."

Even *he* hears that. "Well, if you don't get us gigs, what are you gonna do?"

"I thought I might sit out front and adore you."

He grins. Perfect teeth. Killer cheekbones. People stare at him on the street. Not just girls, either. Women. Moms. Somebody's mom who wants to do I-don't-know-what to him. Maybe just gaze. Maybe get a room at the Hilton and give him a bath, then go home and make a meat loaf for the family.

"Lori, want to fool around?" His eyebrows go up. I must have cartoon-itis today. Everything about him seems exaggerated: hunk of cheese, huge feet, semaphore eyebrows saying hubba-hubba, oh baby, you're the one for me. Crap you'd read on little candy hearts in February.

"Mom gets home about four-thirty."

"So? It's four-fifteen."

"Good for you. You found the big hand."

"Huh?" His mouth goes soft and pouty, like those guys in *GQ*, wearing two-thousand-dollar suits.

I try again. "We don't have time."

He gets up and crawls toward me. His hair hangs down in his eyes so perfect I think he's practiced this. I can imagine him in his room on his hands and knees in front of the big mirror.

This endears him to me. Not that he rehearsed for me. Please. Just that he practiced at all.

He rolls over on his back. Like Pluto. All big and goofy. His tongue lolls out of one side of his mouth.

I lean over him. One eye is bluer than the other. I've got girlfriends who just about pass out when they talk about his eyes. What they're like when he asks to borrow their homework or to front him a couple of bucks.

"You could scratch my tummy," he says.

"Yeah?" I say. "And then what?" They are pretty fantastic. His eyes, I mean. The whites are pure white. Settings for those mismatched jewels. Thank God his breath is cheesy.

All of a sudden he sits up. Bye-bye, love. "Hey, look!" There's another band on TV. "That's the kind of guitar I'm going to get," he says. "When I get one."

◦ ◦ ◦

I have this one girlfriend, and all we talk about is Lincoln. Her name is Tess but I don't think of her as Tess. I think of her as a repository of Lincoln lore. If you rented one of those storage units, would you call it Tess? I think not.

"What'd you guys do?" she asks when she phones this time.

"Came here after school."

"Was your mom home?"

"Nope."

"So?" I can almost hear her squirming. This is like 1-888-LINCOLN. *What was he wearing?*

"I made him a sandwich."

"What kind?"

"Cheese. "

"I love it that he's vegetarian."

He's not vegetarian, but I let that slide.

"Then what?" Tess asks.

"Then he brushed his teeth. We were going to fool around and he wanted his breath to be nice."

"He used your toothbrush?"

"Sure."

I could hear in her voice that if said toothbrush ever turned up on eBay, she'd be the first bidder.

"So then you kissed?"

"Uh-huh."

"What was it like?"

"Like last time."

"Soft at first."

"Yeah."

"But then . . ."

I could put the phone down because Tess is busy writing this bodice ripper with me on the cover sporting bigger boobs, and bare-chested Lincoln astride a lathered-up stallion.

Enough of this. "And then Mom came home."

"After."

"Way after."

"Please!" He's begging, but it's insincere. So insincere that it's almost authentic. "Pretty please." He gets down on one knee like a guy in an old-fashioned ad for engagement rings.

We're in the Pit at school. Junk food dispensers along one wall. Tables with graffiti-proof tops all covered with names and gang signs—who's in love, who's been had, who'd better watch out, who'd better not cry.

People look at Lincoln on his knees and grin. He can get away with anything.

"This could be my big chance." He puts both arms around my legs. The girls think he's doing tragic Heathcliff. To me it's more like a tackle. Like he's bringing me down way short of the goal.

"The photographer will meet us out there. She's got to take pictures of the horsies for some article or something.

Then she'll do me. So you won't have to drive me to Hollywood, to her studio or anything. And it's all free."

"Fine."

The minute I say it, he's on his feet. I can still feel his hands on my legs. But that's over for him. Now he's looking over my shoulder. It's either some freshman in a skirt up to her clavicle or Oreos.

"Got a dollar, babe?"

Oreos. The snack pack.

I don't tell my mom about the racetrack. She hates the place.

"So where are you guys going?" She doesn't look up from the blouse she's ironing.

"Someplace in Arcadia. Photo shoot. Arboretum, maybe."

"Lincoln looks like a model."

"That's what everybody says, so it must be true."

He picks me up in his dad's old Volvo wagon.

"Is this screwed or what?" He scoots over, away from the wheel. He's the only boy I know who doesn't like to drive.

"There's a huge parking lot. She's not gonna see your car. And what if she did? She's passing the pictures on, right? It's not up to her. She's just the photographer."

"What if we all walk out together?"

"We won't."

"What if we do?"

"I'll say it's mine."

He leans back. "The first thing I'm gonna do when I sign is buy a Pontiac Firebird."

"What if I don't want to drive around in a Firebird?"

"Yeah, you do." He doesn't even open his eyes. Then he sticks his arms out the window. "How far is it? Maybe I could get a little tan."

He's thin and pale. An old look if you ask me: heroin-chic. Not that he's an addict. He's not. He smokes a little weed, but everybody smokes a little weed.

I get us on the freeway and point the Daddy-wagon east. There's a baby seat in the back. For Lincoln's little brother, Seth. I know Lincoln's parents. I've had dinner over there. They're nice. Solid. They look at Lincoln like he's another species. He's so not them. They concentrate on Seth.

"Should I be smoking when she sees me the first time?" He lets a cigarette dangle off his lower lip. "Would that be cool?"

I reach over and turn it around so the filter is in his mouth.

"Where'd you get that?"

"Why?"

"It's a Virginia Slim. The Marlboro Man is gonna kick your butt. Would kick your butt if he was alive. Which he isn't."

He tosses the smoke out the window. "I found it, anyway."

Right. In some chick's purse.

The 134 Freeway turns into the 210 around Pasadena, and when I see the San Gabriel Mountains, I start to slide back in time. I've made this drive a thousand times with Dad. Him behind the wheel, me with a Barbie. Yeah, I was that little.

Mom was at work. I was out of school at 2:30. We sat with his buddies. In nonsmoking. Everybody was nice. The guys bought me milk. Kept an eye on me. There was this one sweetheart named Mel who'd had a couple of heart attacks. His cardiologist told him to take naps. So he did. But at the track. There were lots of grassy places. Mel brought a blanket. We'd stop at the bathrooms. Then we'd wander out and snooze. Mel left his bets with the other guys. When we got back to the table, they'd shake their heads mournfully. Mel never won.

Dad did, though. Not all the time, but enough. He knew what he was doing: speed figures, track bias, trainer patterns. He made a living, but it was always boom or bust. And Mom couldn't take it. She's a teacher. Couldn't introduce him as a gambler. Couldn't. And wouldn't lie. Made him choose. Her or it. Us, actually, or it. Bad move, Mom.

"Ever hear from your dad?"

Lincoln's been flirting with a convertible full of Arcadia cuties, so he makes his voice all low and concerned.

"Postcards. Sometimes."

"Is he gonna be out here today?"

"Would he send me a postcard if he was in L.A.?"

He scrunches up his perfect forehead. "He might. To save, like, a phone call."

"He went East."

"It's cool he didn't let your mom tame him."

"Lincoln, he sacrificed me."

"Huh?" He probably sees me tied to a stake while guys with spears dance around me. Then he gives up on that. "Some of us can't breed in captivity."

I'm sick of that line, which he heard on TV and which he uses way too much.

"But he did breed. Otherwise I wouldn't be here."

He squirms. "You know what I mean."

That's the other thing he says: *You know what I mean.* Like I'm a Berlitz girl. Or one of those machines that translates everything at the touch of a button.

I make the turnoff at Baldwin. "The mall?" Lincoln perks up. He gets a lot of attention in a mall. The guy who set him up with this photographer today spotted him in a mall.

I point the other way. "The track."

Lincoln likes it that there are tickets waiting for us at Will Call. In his name. We bump through the turnstile. Automatically I buy a program. I always bought the program. The seller knew me, would lean over and take my dollar. "Good luck, sweetie."

"How many races are there?"

"Eight."

"So the whole thing takes like eight minutes?"

"There's a half-hour between."

"What for?"

"Pageantry."

"Huh?"

"They have to saddle the horses, lead them to the walking ring, warm them up on the backstretch."

That's too much information for Lincoln. "Where's the fountain? Meg said she'd meet us at the fountain."

I could find it with my eyes closed. Mel and I used to nap by the fountain on days when the crowd was light.

Lincoln grabs my arm. "Think that's her?"

"Let's see: spiky red hair, leather jacket even though it's hot as hell, and cameras hanging all over her. What do you think, Sherlock?"

"Hey!" Meg waves and smiles. She's got good teeth, too. Makes me want to go somewhere and floss.

We do the introductions. Meg holds up a light meter, squints at Lincoln. Then me.

"Would you get us some Cokes? I didn't want to not be here when you guys showed up, and I'm really thirsty."

"Sure." I take her twenty, folded the long way.

"And a cheeseburger!" says Guess Who.

I watch her lead Lincoln toward a topiary horse. She stands him up; he slouches and sneers. She scowls. "Don't try so hard."

I go toward El Mercado, climb a dozen steps. Everything's the same: lines at the windows, lights on the odds board, and all around a kind of grumbly white noise.

Inside the snack bar, I load a little cardboard tray. The cashier glances at me, punches numbers, glances again.

"Did you used to come here a long time ago? With your dad, maybe? You liked the frozen malts, right?"

"My god." I look at her nametag. It's Mabel. Ageless Mabel.

"Honey, how are you?"

"I'm good."

"How's your dad?"

That's what she really wants to know. "He's dead."

Out comes her hand. Bejeweled. "Oh, sweetie. And he was so handsome."

Mabel cancels everything on her register and gives me the food. For old times' sake.

Out the door I go. I glance at the board. I hear the announcer call the horses' names as they get to the gate. I put the food down, get out my program, glance at the ladder of names. Number seven is named Irreconcilable. There's almost nobody in line to bet now. Why not.

Walking away from the window, I'm almost alone. The action is in the other direction—past the betting windows, the beer stands, the double doors to the huge, groomed oval. Down by the paddock where I'm headed there's nobody except a few girlfriends or moms reading. There's Meg walking around Lincoln, taking thirty pictures a minute.

I slow down, listen to the call of the race. The crowd gets into it when the horses turn for home, that big wave of longing. Then it's over. A few women squeal. The real players grin or turn the page.

I walk up to Meg and Lincoln, let them choose their goodies. Then I show them my ticket.

"I won."

Lincoln stops chewing. "Really? How much?"

I glance at the board, do the math. "Sixty." I look at Meg. "I bet with your money. What was left of that twenty." Which was the whole thing, thanks to Mabel.

Meg has a very slanty grin. Precipitous. I'm used to translating for Lincoln, so I know what it means: *I shouldn't have asked you to run errands but I was hot and thirsty. You shouldn't have agreed. But since you did, it's cool you spent the money.*

Lincoln gobbles his cheeseburger. "When am I gonna hear, Meg?"

"Not up to me." She's looking at me, talking to him. Toward him. "I just take the pictures."

"But when?"

I step in. "She doesn't know, Lincoln."

He wipes his fingers on his shirt. "Let's bet again."

"Sure, why not."

"Yeah," says Meg. "It's only my money."

I betrayed her by siding with him.

"Let's look at the horses."

He tugs at me. "So c'mon."

"They're not out yet."

"So where are they?"

I point. "In the saddling paddock."

"Getting dressed? All right! Peep show." He gallops off.

"How do you know about this?" Meg asks.

"I used to come with my dad."

"Where is he?"

"Nursing home." I like putting him in different scenarios. A little toy dad I can do what I want with.

Meg settles on a bench, shrugs off her equipment, lets her practiced eye run the length of the grandstand. "It's an interesting place. You're an interesting girl."

I pick up on the first part. "Downstairs in the Keg Room very pale people watch everything on closed-circuit TV. They eat strange food they bring themselves. If somebody buys a beer and leaves it to go bet, when they get back the beer is gone and the plastic cup has a bite out of it. Upstairs is the Turf Club: guy in a tuxedo with his hand out. Coats and ties. Everybody smells good."

I take a breath. "In between lie the rest of us. Oh, yeah, let's not forget Mexico." I point toward the barns. "Hot walkers and grooms. Every *corazon* a broken one. Knife fights on Saturday night."

Meg sighs. "Little stereotypical, don't you think?"

"And you're not, with your leather jacket and nasty little boots?"

She's about to say something when the outrider leads the field into the walking ring. I stand up, head that way. Meg joins me.

The first filly is all lathered up, sweat dripping off her belly. Right behind her is a big chestnut with a blaze on her face. Her coat is good but she's built to go long and this race is short.

"What are you looking for?" Meg is right beside me, her arm against mine.

"Inspiration."

The number-five horse has a nice way about her but when I glance at her name on the program, Foolish Bahama, I lose interest. It's a made-up name, partly from her sire, partly from her mom. No imagination.

Lincoln lopes up. "This is so cool!"

Everybody shushes him, and a tough guy calls him a name.

Lincoln grins, acts chastised. "This is so cool." Big
stage whisper.

Then I see number nine: ears pricked, curious but
composed. I watch her walk away from me. There's not a
drop of kidney sweat. I point to her name, Brutal Interlude, and Meg grins. But Lincoln frowns. He doesn't
know *interlude*.

We wander toward the windows with everybody else.
Their heads are bent like monks in some cold scriptorium.

"Let me do it," Lincoln says. "I want to vote."

"It's bet."

"Let me bet." He holds out his hand.

"What's the horse's name?"

"Huh?"

"What number is she?" Meg joins in.

I just head for the windows.

"Bet all to win. Go for it, Lori!"

I get in line, bet the sixty dollars. I can hear Lincoln
behind me. "Come on, Big Interview! Come on!" He's
got the name wrong; post time is five minutes away. But
it doesn't matter. With just minutes to the break, everybody's a little nuts.

Meg lassos me with her eyes. "Where's the bathroom?
Come with me."

We park Lincoln by a big red pole, make him promise to stay there. "Or no TV later," I say like a mom.
Then I lead Meg toward the elevator.

Downstairs through the pink double doors, nothing's changed. Long lines of little café chairs. Long mirrors. Then through another door to the toilets.

Meg takes a few pictures. The old ladies smile back at us in the mirrors. They're wearing serious rouge.

Meg doesn't pee; she just washes her hands. She talks to my reflection.

"Your boyfriend's not going to make it. He's pretty enough, but the camera hates him." Then she shrugs and takes a towel from the attendant, a white lady in this enlightened age. I tip her a buck, like I was taught.

"Or maybe it's just me." Meg picks up her little camera. "He just works my nerves." She gets me in her viewfinder, snaps. "What are you doing with him, anyway?"

"Reflected glory, if it's any of your business."

She lowers the Nikon. "I go to this private club in Silverlake. You don't have to be twenty-one to listen to the music." Significant glance. "Or dance."

"What's the next question: Have I ever read Sappho? Am I open to new experiences?"

"He treats you crappy."

"He's not the one who sent me to the store for snacks. You didn't even say please."

She turns away.

⊙ ⊙ ⊙

Upstairs, Lincoln is gone. Of course.

Meg offers, "Want me to help you find him?"

She's mad but the supplication bleeds through. The beseeching. I get enough of that from yon Missing Person.

"He'll turn up. I've got the car keys."

"I'm out of here. Take care." She puts her arms around me. I pat her equipment bag.

Then I take a little walk. Huge banners with jockeys' pictures hang from the ceiling. The top three or four riders. Plus Shoemaker and Arcaro: the legends.

It's less than a minute to the post. Guys in the back of the line grumble. Then I spot Lincoln. He's chatting up the girl who peddles hand-carved sandwiches, leaning into her station farther than he should. She's plain, with spots on her apron. She's making him a sandwich with two kinds of meat.

I walk right up. "Are you flirting again, you bastard? What did I tell you about that? What did I say I'd do next time?"

He's flustered. She goes dead pale and kind of waves her knife at me. Then I laugh.

Now she's bewildered. Lincoln snorts, grabs his sandwich. "Dude," he says, "what's with you?"

"I'm pretending to give a shit."

I lead him out front. The race goes off.

"What's happening?" Lincoln bounces up and down. "Are we winning?"

In fact, we are. I can see the cherry silks of Brutal Interlude. She's moving smoothly, four wide but in the clear. I'm a long way from the turn but I know what's happening. Dad and I used to stand there and watch them change leads, lay back their ears, and go for the wire.

"Is that him? Did we win?"

"Yeah."

"All right!" Everything flies out of Lincoln's sandwich. People look up like it's a plague *(and in the latter days, meat—mostly white meat but a little corned beef—shall fall from the heavens).* Then they locate the source and scowl.

"What'd we win? How much?"

I glance at the board. "Couple of hundred."

"Babe!" Now he wants to kiss me. Now.

I push him away. "You're all greasy."

"Let's bet again. One more time and we can buy that guitar." He tugs at my hand. "C'mon."

"Go ahead. I'll meet you. I'm going to the bathroom."

"You just went."

"I'll meet you by the fountain."

Downstairs I wash my face, glance in the mirror. I'm not bad looking. Better than that sandwich girl.

There's a racing newspaper on the green couch. I sit down and find the next race. Each horse has a biography of its own. A curriculum vitae. Some are chronicles of success. Others are case studies for the indifferent or injured. I look for the one I want.

Outside on the grass, Lincoln is playing with a baby. Its mom is maybe twenty. In a red tube top. When I walk up, she gets a little weird. "Who are you? I'm Candy."

"I'm his sister."

"Oh, okay. Good. 'Cause he told me—"

"Arthur? It's time for your medication."

Candy frowns. Frowning Candy says, "He said his name was Lincoln."

I nod. "That's why it's time for the blue pill."

Lincoln follows me. "What's with you today, babe? You're far out. Are you on something?" His arm snakes around my waist. "Have you got a little for Lincoln?"

"Let's look at these horses."

They parade past us. I can hear my dad. "If you get a hit on somebody, honey, tell me." He never asked me unless he was in trouble. Almost broke. I'm maybe nine. And I'm supposed to get *him* out for the day.

"Which one is ours?" Lincoln is whispering in my ear. It turns me on a little. The body as quisling. The body as foe.

"Number seven. Short Circuit."

He's a mild-looking old gelding. This is his job. He's done it almost a hundred times.

"Are you sure?"

"Have I been wrong yet?"

"I want to bet this time. Please."

I lead him to the windows. "Give the clerk this ticket. He'll put it through the machine and say, 'Do you want to bet?' You say, 'Put it all on number seven.' Okay?"

I watch him fidget in line. He keeps glancing over his shoulder, making sure I'm there. Then he plays some air guitar. He bets and gallops back to me.

"How much are we gonna win?"

"Short Circuit's twenty-to-one. That's forty for two dollars. Four hundred for twenty. We bet a hundred and fifty."

Lincoln's eyes get wide. He can't do the math but he knows it's a lot. "Bah da dah dum. Da dah da dum. Dah DUM." He strums his thigh. Takes a bow.

Like I knew he would, Short Circuit runs fourth almost all the way. Then he tires in the lane and finishes sixth.

Lincoln is stunned. "We didn't win."

I dig in my purse. Hand him the keys. "Here."

"No. You drive." He's staring at the numbers on the board, checking the ticket in his hand. "What happened? Now we can't buy my guitar."

"You're on your own."

It starts to register. "Are you kidding? I don't even know where I am."

"Get on the freeway. Go east."

"What's the matter with you?"

I turn my back on him.

"Hey!"

I keep walking.

"You bitch."

I've got this fifty-dollar bill Mom gave me for emergencies. So I walk toward the line of taxis. All the drivers are standing under a palm tree, lying about gas mileage and blonds.

I give my program to an old guy on his way in. He's very polite. He tips his hat. He says, "Thank you." He calls me Miss.

That's more like it.

ABOUT THE AUTHOR

Lively dialogue and interesting characters are earmarks of Ron Koertge's short stories and novels, which include *Where the Kissing Never Stops* and *Confess-O-Rama*. His *Tiger, Tiger, Burning Bright* was named a Blue Ribbon Book by the *Bulletin of the Center for Children's Books,* a Bank Street Children's Book of the Year, a Judy Lopez Memorial Award Honor Book, and an American Library Association Best Book for Young Adults. The American

Library Association considers his *The Arizona Kid* one of the 100 Best of the Best Books for Young Adults published between 1967 and 1992.

When he's not writing or teaching at the city college in Pasadena, California, Ron Koertge often heads for the local race-track—horses, not cars. While driving the freeway to Arcadia, where Santa Anita is, he thought, "Say, this is a journey!" At the same time, he says, he was in the mood to write a story about a sassy girl. And so Lori and her experiences intersected with horse racing—"Brutal Interlude" is the result.

In *The Brimstone Journals*, Ron Koertge combines his poetic talent with his insights into teenagers. That novel is composed of poems written from the points of view of fifteen students, revealing the longing, anger, and intolerance in their high school and the resulting violence that might erupt at any time. His most recent novel is called *Stoner & Spaz*.

❉

It's a very short trip from the church to the diner in town,
but the lesson Tommy learns at the diner means a lot
more than what he learned during the sermon.

Bread on the Water

David Lubar

"It's going to be a long sermon," Andy whispered to me.

"Yeah, we're doomed." I could tell we were in trouble all the way from the back pew. Pastor Donald had stuck so many little colored slips of paper in his Bible, it looked like a piñata. He wasn't the sort of preacher who'd share a couple short verses and set us free to enjoy the day. He really liked to hammer home his messages.

"Turn with me to Romans twelve," Pastor Donald said.

Andy started to snicker. "Romans twelve, Christians nothing," he whispered.

"Ssshhh." I gave him an elbow and looked around. Mrs. Skeffington, three pews ahead and over to the left, was glaring at us. So were Mr. and Mrs. Linden, over on the right.

"As most of you are aware," Pastor Donald said, "this is one of Paul's most important epistles."

"Is the epistle loaded?" Andy asked.

I knew I shouldn't have sat back here with Andy. But I liked hanging out with him. Except when he got goofy. Which was more than half the time. Right now, he'd buried his face in his hands. I could hear snorts spilling out as he tried to muffle the laughter.

"Knock it off, Andy," I said. "It wasn't that funny."

Pastor Donald started to read out loud. "Verse twenty tells us, 'if your enemy is hungry, feed him.' "

"Feed him some knuckles," Andy said, lifting his face from his hands.

I checked out my parents, up front. They hadn't looked back. Not yet. Neither had Andy's parents. If I could just get Andy to calm down, everything would be okay. "Just cut it out," I said. "All right?"

No such luck. Andy was on a roll. And Pastor Donald was about to hand him even better material to work with. After a brief visit with the Good Samaritan in Luke, and a short hop through Ecclesiastes, he landed squarely in James, chapter two, verse fifteen.

" 'If a brother or sister be naked . . .' "

"If a sister be naked, I'm staying," Andy said. "If a brother be naked, I'm splitting."

" '. . . and destitute of daily food . . .' "

"I thought destitutes made good money." He scratched his head. "Hold it. I think I got my 'tutes mixed up."

" 'And one of you say unto them, Depart in peace, be ye warmed and filled; notwithstanding ye give them not those things which are needful to the body; what doth it profit?' "

"Doth?" Andy said, stretching it out wetly like Daffy Duck. "Doth who? Doth Vader?" He looked at me and raised one eyebrow. "Be ye warm, Tommy?"

As I reached over to smack Andy, the shadow of Assistant Pastor John fell across us.

"Out," he whispered, pointing at the door with one hand and clutching the edge of the pew with the other. I could almost hear the wood splintering beneath his grip.

"I wasn't doing anything," I said.

His index finger curled in, joining the rest of his fist. "Out. Both of you."

Andy shrugged and slipped past me. I followed him toward the door, hoping nobody noticed that we'd just been banished from church. As I glanced back, I saw that Mrs. Skeffington was following our exodus with the gloating satisfaction of someone who has just seen her worst enemy caught stealing money from the collection plate. No doubt, she'd make sure that my parents didn't remain uninformed of my transgression.

My only consolation was the sight of Pastor Donald's Bible, which still had enough slips in it to fuel a small fire. I was going to miss a ton of Scripture.

I could still hear Pastor Donald as the door closed behind me. "We are here to help others. Friend, enemy, brother, sister, neighbor, stranger—it doesn't matter."

Apparently, Andy could hear him, too. "Butcher, baker, candlestick maker," he said, getting in one last shot.

I pushed him, but not too hard. It felt good to be free.

"So, whatcha want to do?" Andy asked when we'd walked down the steps to the street.

"I want to snap your head off," I said.

"Now that's not very Christian." Andy pointed over his shoulder. "You should spend more time in church."

"Look who's talking." I wanted to be angry, but what the heck—it was a beautiful autumn day, cold and crisp, without a cloud in the sky. And my fate was at least an hour and a half away. Between the sermon and the singing, church wouldn't get out until eleven. I slipped into my jacket.

Andy was already walking toward the center of town. "What do you feel like doing?" I asked when I'd caught up with him.

"I don't know. How much money you got?"

I looked through my wallet. "Enough for a couple orders of fries and some shakes," I said. "But not enough for a cruise to the Bahamas."

"Guess we'll have to settle for the fries." Andy checked his own wallet. "I think I can upgrade our meal in the direction of a couple burgers."

We headed toward the Bridgeview Diner. When we were half a block away, I noticed a guy huddled in the entrance of a small office building across the street. He noticed me, too. He stood and headed toward us in a way that reminded me of how my cat acts when I open the fridge.

"Man, he's going to ask for spare change," I said. His hand was already out. I hated dealing with bums.

"I never give them money," Andy said.

I was glad to hear that. I figured they probably just spent it on booze.

Sure enough, the guy reached us before we could get to the door of the diner. I took a step back. He looked pretty grubby. His wool plaid jacket was so worn that the squares were all the same color. I dropped my gaze and found myself staring at shoes that had split on the sides and were now wrapped with twine. "Could you boys spare some money? I haven't eaten in a while." His voice was so quiet I almost couldn't make out the words.

Before I could tell him to leave us alone, Andy said, "I'd be happy to buy you some food. You want a meal? Come with us."

I glanced at Andy, surprised. But then I figured out what he was doing. He was calling the guy's bluff. That was brilliant. The bum didn't want food. He wanted our money so he could go buy a bottle of cheap wine. No way he'd come with us.

"After you," Andy said, holding the door open.

The guy went in. Man, I'd have bet a million bucks he'd have walked away from the offer. I figured Andy would back off now, but he followed the man right in. I didn't. I was used to Andy doing what he wanted. I'd seen him do stuff at school—like talk with the kids who everyone else made fun of. But this was way over the top. Whoever the joke was on, it wasn't funny.

I thought about splitting. No way I wanted to eat with this guy. I glanced at my watch. It was too early to go back to church. Besides, I couldn't ditch Andy. He'd stuck with me a couple times when it would have been more fun to take off. And he was the only one from our school who'd visited me back when I'd had my appendix out. On the other hand, I'd never made him share a meal with a bum. "Let's just get it over with," I muttered as I went through the door.

The place wasn't exactly fancy. Even so, the waitress gave all three of us the same sort of look I'd probably just given the guy myself. I guess she'd already figured she wasn't in for much of a tip from two kids and a bum. She turned away from us and fidgeted with the coffee pot, then started wiping the counter with a rag.

We grabbed a booth. I slid in next to Andy. I didn't really want to face the guy, but it beat sitting next to him.

Andy pointed to himself. "I'm Andy. This is Tommy."

The man nodded toward Andy, then toward me, but he kept his eyes down and didn't tell us his name. His left hand was shaking. After a minute, he put it on his lap.

The waitress finally came over. "Ready?" she asked, her pad out and pencil poised. I guess she didn't want to invest too much effort in conversation.

"After you," Andy said to our guest.

The guy looked at the menu, but didn't speak.

"Get whatever you want," Andy said. "It's our treat."

Our treat? I shot Andy a look. He shrugged, as if he assumed I wouldn't mind. I guess there wasn't anything I could do about it right now. And he'd sprung for a movie last month when I was broke, so it sort of worked out.

The guy glanced up at the waitress, then back at the menu. I thought about the times when someone was treating me and I wasn't sure how much they wanted to spend. I always wrestled with what to get.

The waitress cleared her throat, then sighed. I didn't see why she was in such a rush. There weren't any other customers at the moment except for one guy at the counter, eating a donut.

"How about a steak and a salad?" Andy suggested.

The man nodded. In my head, I could hear the *kaching* of the cash register.

"Cokes for us," Andy added. He glanced at me. "Split some fries?"

I shook my head. "I'm not hungry."

The waitress scritched her pencil across the pad, then left.

"Thank you," the man said.

"Our pleasure," Andy said. "Me and Tommy, we've known each other since we were little. I'm a jock. Tommy wants to be, but he's pretty uncoordinated. They let him on some of the teams because they feel sorry for him." He glanced out the window. "Nice day, today. Supposed to be sunny the rest of the week. I noticed they're tearing up part of Main Street for the new parking garage."

Andy kept talking, stopping once in a while to allow the guy to say something if he wanted to, but not asking any questions. I guess Andy talked because that's what people do when they're waiting for their food. And I guess the guy didn't talk because it was hard enough just asking for the food. I wondered how many people had turned him down today. And I wondered how he'd ended up on the street. This close, beneath the whiskers and the dirt, he could pass for one of my uncles. Actually, I had an uncle who looked worse. For that matter, I had an aunt with more whiskers, too.

It was starting to sink in that this wasn't any kind of joke. This was just Andy being himself. Of course, if his act of kindness annoyed the waitress, I suspected that was just fine with him, too.

I could smell the steak before it came out of the kitchen. My stomach rumbled, even though I'd stuffed myself on pancakes at breakfast. A whole hour ago. Across the room, the donut eater tossed a couple of coins on the counter and headed up front to pay his bill.

A moment later, the waitress came out of the kitchen. She plopped down the thick white plate with a loud clack, then gave us our sodas.

The guy tore into the food, eating so fast at first, I was afraid he'd choke. He finally slowed after half the steak and all of the salad had vanished. No question, he'd been hungry. I sipped my soda and thought about how lucky I was to have a home and a family. Even a family that dragged me to church every Sunday.

Andy kept talking. I talked some, too. The guy didn't talk, but he looked at each of us now as we spoke. I didn't look away when he caught my eye. I tried to imagine who he'd been. Tried to really see him.

Lifting his right hand, he pointed to the pile of French fries on his plate.

"Hey, thanks, don't mind if I do," Andy said. He reached out and grabbed a couple.

He nudged me. I took one and ate it. It didn't kill me. Actually, it tasted pretty good. The three of us sat there and shared the rest of the fries.

The waitress was back the instant the guy swallowed his last bite. I still hadn't finished my soda. "Pay there," she said, putting the bill down by Andy's glass and tilting her head toward the register. I gave him all my cash and he went up front.

"Thank you," the guy said as he stood.

"You're welcome."

He started to leave, then turned back and held out his hand. We shook. His grip was firmer than I expected. He headed out, stopping by Andy for a moment. They shook hands, too. Andy came back as I slurped the last of my drink. I saw he still had some money. He jammed a dollar in my shirt pocket. "Can't let my best friend walk around flat broke." Then he dropped the rest of the money on the table. Three dollars and eighty cents.

"What was that for?" I asked as we left the diner.

"Tip," he said. "She works hard. This place is open all night. She's probably been here since four."

"She wasn't very friendly," I said.

"Would a small tip make her more friendly?" he asked. I guess he had a point.

We walked back through town, reaching the church just as the crowd was coming out the door. I worked my way against the flow, hoping to hook up with my parents before they figured out I hadn't been there during the service.

"I'm toast," I muttered to Andy as I caught sight of Mrs. Skeffington talking to my mom.

When my folks reached me, my dad didn't waste any time. "I'm very disappointed with you," he said.

"Sorry."

"Getting thrown out of a church service. Of all the places to misbehave." He went on for a while, and I nodded and made the proper noises to show how bad I felt. Out of the corner of my eye, I could see Andy dancing through the same routine with his mom and dad.

Finally, my dad turned to my mom and said, "Let's go. I'm starving."

I followed my parents to the car and got inside. Behind us, I saw old Mrs. Wilming hobbling slowly along the sidewalk. Mrs. Skeffington cruised past her, not offering a ride. On the church steps, the Lindens were pulling their little kid by the arms as he dragged his feet and screamed his head off, pleading for a Happy Meal. When they reached level ground, Mrs. Linden gave him a swat on the rear to speed him along. Through my open window, I heard her say, "Just wait till I get you home."

"We're trying to raise you the right way," my mom said as Dad shot out of the parking lot. "We want you to have some decent values. Not like that friend of yours."

"But he's—"

"Drop it," Dad warned before I could say anything to defend Andy.

I sighed and settled back in my seat. Dad cursed as he got caught in town by the long red light on Harmony Street. To my right, I saw the waitress from the diner. I guess she was on her way home. A guy in a long overcoat walked up to her, his hand out. She stopped and reached into her pocket.

The light changed and we drove off. I looked back, but I didn't get to see what happened. Maybe she gave him something. I'd like to think so.

In the front seats, my parents were playing Invisible Son, talking about me like I wasn't there.

"Tommy needs to show better judgment. That Andy kid is a bad influence," my dad said.

My mom nodded. "Teaching our son all the wrong things. Running around, getting into trouble. And his mother. Did you see the dress she was wearing? It was so tacky."

"We'll straighten Tommy out," my dad said. He floored the gas and tried to beat the next light. It was red by the time he went through it. "I'm gonna make goddam sure he doesn't skip any more sermons. Somebody's got to teach him right from wrong. I'll tell you something else. Next Sunday, he's sitting up front with us. We'll see he doesn't miss anything."

I reached into my shirt pocket and took out the dollar bill Andy had given me. As my parents continued to discuss the lessons I was going to learn, I held the bill near the window and let the breeze tug at it, then loosened my grip and watched it fly free.

ABOUT THE AUTHOR

"I'm a compulsive short story writer," says David Lubar. "I've tried to cut down, but I haven't been able to quit completely." Good thing for us readers. "Bread on the Water," he says, started with nothing more than the thought of two guys fooling around in the back of a church. "The story just developed as I set them free and watched what they did."

Writing realistic fiction is not the norm for this author. He usually chooses to write about giant slugs, zombies, werewolves, and monstrous creatures . . . all in fun, however. His books include *The Vanishing Vampire, The Unwilling Witch, The Wavering Werewolf,* and *The Gloomy Ghost* as well as *Monster Road* and two PsychoZone short story anthologies: *Kidzilla and Other Tales* and *The Witch's Monkey and Other Tales.* His most highly praised work is *Hidden Talents,* a novel about a group of boys in a last-chance type of school who discover they have very special abilities. That novel was chosen by the American Library Association as a Best Book for Young Adults as well as a Quick Pick.

In addition to his own special writing talent, David Lubar has been an editor of a computer magazine and a designer and programmer of video games, among them Frogger 2 for the GameBoy. His latest novels include *The Trouble with Heroes* and *Dunk.*

David Lubar's website—www.davidlubar.com—will tell you more.

Lindley, who has never been farther away from Pine Hollow than the Wal-Mart in the next town, is on her way to a special summer program at college for high-achieving high school students. Is she smart enough and savvy enough to compete?

My People

Margaret Peterson Haddix

The people in my family aren't the kind who ever go anywhere. So when that letter came in the fall, I knew it didn't make any sense to go getting my hopes up.

But as Granny always says, hope and sense aren't exactly kissing cousins. My hopes went shooting up like a firecracker on the Fourth of July. I read that letter again and again, near fifty times, until I could close my eyes and see the words in my head.

Dear Ms. Havens:

Congratulations! As the top scorer in your region on the state aptitude test, you are cordially invited to participate in the College for High Schoolers at Mercer University, July 12–19. Join in college-level seminars with the best and brightest in the state. Learn from Mercer's world-class faculty. Experience the finest in Mercer's state-of-the-art facilities. . . .

The rest of the letter got into specifics, like what kind of sleeping bag to bring. I thought it was fascinating reading, the way *Soap Opera Digest* was for my aunt Eugenia.

Should I just mention right here that nobody in my family had ever gone to college? We heard tell that one of my third cousins, Bobby Ray Brighton, stepped foot on a community college campus once, but he was just lost. Should I mention that Mercer University was four, maybe five hours away, and I'd never been any farther from home than the Wal-Mart over in Spikesville?

If you know those couple of facts, you'll know why I hid that letter in the bottom of my underwear drawer for a week. I took it out every morning to read, just in case the words might have changed in the night. But I never showed it to anyone. Who was I going to show it to?

My parents would have said, "Well, that's real nice, honey," and gone back to watching reruns of *The Price Is Right.* It never would have occurred to them that I might want to *go* to this College for High Schoolers.

My teachers would have been proud enough, but they would have held the letter up for the whole school to see. "Look, you all, and see what Lindley went and did! See what you can accomplish with a little studying and hard work?" And all the other kids would have looked at me like I'd grown an extra head, like I belonged with the bearded lady and the miniature man at the county fair.

If I'd shown my friends—well, see above.

But there was Granny . . .

Granny had dropped out of school in about fifth grade. Still, if there was any sort of degree out there in listening, she would have deserved one.

So on a Sunday afternoon when everyone else in my house seemed to be taking naps, I sneaked down the hill to Granny's. I wanted to thrust the letter at her and let her read it for herself, but between her bad eyes, her bad glasses the welfare office never gets around to replacing, and that dropping out of school all those years ago, she's not much for reading. So I read the letter out loud. I read her everything, even the part about sleeping bags.

"Always knew you were smart," she said when I was done.

"I'm good at taking tests," I said. "Daddy'll tell you that's not the same thing."

Daddy often did tell me—and anyone else who would listen. "Hear about my girl?" he'd brag down at Sippers Bar. "I never did know what A's on a report card looked like, until I saw one of hers. But she forgot to put gas in the lawn mower last week, ran it com-plete-ly dry. Maybe ruined the motor. And she forgot to put baking powder in, last time she made biscuits. If that's smart, I'm sure glad I'm stupid."

I did do a whole bunch of stupid things, so I could hardly blame Daddy for questioning my intelligence. But hand me one of those test papers where you fill in little circles with a No. 2 pencil, and I was right at home. Even if I didn't have a clue what the question was about, it was like my hand and the pencil would know which little circle to darken. Granny says some of our ancestors were the kind of people who could discover water by holding on to a willow branch and walking around—dousing, it's called. Maybe I inherited some of that. Pencils, willow switches—both are wood, right? And those little-circle answers are about as valuable now as water was back a hundred years ago, aren't they?

I think I just made up an analogy. Lord, those little-circle tests love analogies.

"The state thinks you're smart," Granny said, like that settled the question. She rocked a little bit, staring out her living room window at the mountain that rose up smack in front of her driveway. "So you gonna frame this letter and hang it on the wall, or you gonna do something about it?"

That's Granny. She's good at getting right to the point.

I squirmed on Granny's sunk-in couch, which I can remember sitting on as far back as when I was two.

"Well, I *want* to," I said. "I'd give anything to go to

College for High Schoolers. I reckon it'd be like—like heaven. But how am I going to get there? How am I going to pay for it? I mean, I don't even own a sleeping bag!"

"Seems like one of my cousins has a sleeping bag," Granny said. "Now, if I could just remember which one. . . . And you've got nine months to raise the money. If God can make a baby in that amount of time, you ought to be able to make enough money for college. As for getting you there—why, I'll take you. I always did want to see a little bit more of the world before I die."

I stared at Granny. She had a beat-up pickup truck sitting in her driveway—well, who didn't, around here. But I'd never seen her drive it. If she ever needed anything down at the store, we'd pick it up for her, or we'd take her along with us.

"But, but—" I kind of sputtered.

"Now, don't you worry," Granny said. "I can drive fine. Just never had a reason to do much of it before. What do you say?"

What I wanted to say was, "But I didn't tell you about the biggest obstacle of all. How can *I* go to that big fancy university? How can I pull up a chair beside all those really smart kids from all over the state? Don't you know I'm scared out of my shoes of making a fool of myself?" But how could I mention a little thing like terror when Granny was willing to drive for the first time in years?

◦   ◦   ◦

I don't know how long nine months feels for pregnant ladies, but those nine months I spent waiting for the College for High Schoolers couldn't seem to decide whether to drag or fly by. I'd read the letter again and get excited all over again, and it'd seem like all the clocks in the world had just plain stopped. Then I'd get hit with a fit of nerves, and it'd seem like two or three days would zip by while I was just standing there, telling my heart to quit pounding.

When I got excited, I'd beg for extra hours working at McDonald's or I'd go help Granny tinker on her truck. We had it running pretty strong by January, but we kept having to fine-tune it.

When I got nervous, I'd walk down to the library to study so I'd be ready for Mercer University. I read or reread every book there that might be the slightest bit educational—even Jacqueline Susann's *Valley of the Dolls*, because its jacket claimed it was "a pop classic." And I read the library's *Time* magazine from cover to cover every week. You wouldn't believe all the things that were going on in the world outside Pine Hollow.

And then suddenly it was July.

On July 12, all my relatives came by to tell Granny and me goodbye. I think some of them thought they'd never see us again. And I think some of my uncles had a little bet going about whether or not we'd go through with our plum fool plan. Still, it was quite a sight, all those arms waving at us as we drove away. It made me think of people seeing the *Titanic* off, cheering and yelling, and no one knowing an iceberg lay right ahead.

I tried not to think about it.

Granny and I were both quiet for a long while, chugging down the mountain. I hugged the sleeping bag I'd borrowed from my cousin Edna, once removed. My feet rested on the suitcase I'd borrowed from my uncle Floyd. Suddenly it seemed like I was bringing my family with me, not just their things. I felt a little better.

"Look," Granny said softly.

It was the Leaving Spikesville sign, right at the edge of the Wal-Mart parking lot. The road curved ahead, leading places I'd never been.

"New territory," I breathed. I thought of Christopher Columbus, Ferdinand Magellan, Vasco da Gama—any one of those explorers we studied in school. I wished I'd never learned that some of them came to a bad end. Was it Sir Francis Drake or Sir Walter Raleigh who got beheaded by his own people?

We drove around the curve.

"Doesn't look much different," Granny said, sounding a little disappointed. I felt relieved. Every tuft of familiar-looking weeds, every rock-faced mountain, and every falling-down tobacco barn we drove past reminded me I wasn't *that* far from home.

But before very long the scenery changed. The land flattened out, and I could see from horizon to horizon. It made me nervous, being able to see so far ahead of me. I missed the mountains protecting me.

But mostly it was just cornfields around me. I knew about cornfields.

Granny pulled onto a four-lane divided highway, a grand thing. Inside of five minutes, we had a police car behind us, its siren blaring and lights flashing.

"I wasn't speeding, officer," Granny said after we'd pulled over and the policeman strode up to our truck.

"No, you weren't," the policeman agreed. "You were barely going twenty-five. You could get squashed like a bug, driving like that on the highway. Let me see your license, registration, and insurance card."

Granny didn't budge.

"Let me guess," the policeman said. "You don't have any of those."

"Could I speak to you privately, officer?" Granny said.

The policeman shrugged. Granny opened her door and stepped out. Flecks of rust came off where the door rubbed. We never had gotten that fixed perfectly.

Granny slammed the door and she and the policeman walked back toward his car. I sat still, staring forward, concentrating hard. Whatever happened, I was not going to let that policeman see me cry.

Cars whizzed by, and I felt like every single person was staring at me. They probably thought Granny and I were the Beverly Hillbillies. "I got the highest score in my region on the state aptitude test," I wanted to shout out the window. "I'm on my way to *college*."

I dared to turn around and look at Granny and the policeman. The policeman was shaking his head.

Maybe I wasn't on my way to college.

A few minutes later, Granny came back to the truck. She slid into the driver's seat. I turned around and saw the policeman getting back in his car, too. He drove away with a little toot of the siren in farewell.

"What happened?" I asked Granny.

"I know his grandmother," Granny said. She turned the key in the ignition and pulled back onto the highway. I think she started humming then, too, but maybe it was just the engine.

"What about the next policeman we see?" I asked. "What if it's someone you don't know?"

Granny frowned.

"It's no use worrying about the future," Granny said. "That'll just give you a stomachache."

Still, the next time one of those exit signs loomed ahead of us, Granny slowed down and pulled off. We were on windier roads now, driving through dusty little towns.

"Scenic route," Granny said. She gave me a look that kept me from protesting.

In the next hour, we drove through Chalmersburg, Mitchell, Good Egg, Peeveysville, and Silo. I collected places like beads on a string. I planned to remember always the little kid who waved at me in Good Egg, the crooked sidewalks in Silo, the stately dome on the courthouse in Peeveysville. Would I dare talk about any of those with the other kids at Mercer University? Could I mention casually, "Well, when I was driving through Chalmersburg . . ."?

No. Probably all the other kids had been to New York, Los Angeles, London, Paris—real places. Places *Time* magazine mentioned all the time.

What did I think I was doing?

I shouldn't have wondered that. It was bad luck. Just as the last panicky flutter of that thought wiggled through my mind, the engine of Granny's truck gave a little cough and died.

"Oops," Granny said.

She turned the key again, pumped the accelerator. Nothing happened. Granny waited a minute so she wouldn't flood the engine. Then she tried again. Nothing. And again. Nothing.

We both sat still for a minute, listening to the silence. Or not really silence—all sorts of bugs and birds were sawing and singing in the fields around us.

All the bird song sounded like mourning doves to me.

"Guess Uncle Eldon won the bet," I said. He was the one who said we'd never make it.

"Don't give up now, child," Granny said.

She got out—displacing more rust from the door— and opened the hood. We were right in the middle of the road, but that didn't seem to matter. There wasn't any traffic. I slipped out and went to stand beside her.

"Radiator?" I asked.

Granny nodded. "Totally shot."

"Would now be a good time to give up?" I asked.

"Don't be a smart mouth," Granny said. "There's a house up ahead. We can go and call back to that last town—what was it? Spindler? Get the truck towed, have the radiator replaced."

But Granny and I both knew that towing and radiators cost money. Probably more money than we had, even if I threw in my entire College for High Schoolers fund.

Somebody honked a horn at us, one of those big, nasty semitruck horns. I looked around the raised hood and saw a monster of a truck barreling down toward us. It braked with a screech. The driver leaned out the window and hollered, "Get off the road!"

"Why don't you help push?" Granny yelled back.

The driver grumbled back at her, but he left his truck rumbling by the side of the road and climbed down.

Up close, I could see the man was huge, with a long grizzled beard and tattoos up and down his arms. He reminded me a lot of my daddy, and for a second I almost felt homesick, almost didn't mind that I wasn't going to make it to College for High Schoolers. Getting back home would be good enough for me.

Almost.

"What's the problem?" the trucker growled.

"Radiator blew out," Granny said.

The man looked at our truck. "When did that happen? Nineteen seventy-five?"

"Just now," Granny said. "I was taking my granddaughter here to college. College, you know?"

The trucker looked at me for a long time. I don't think he was admiring my brains.

"Up at Mercer?" he asked. "Just so happens I'm heading that way. Want me to take her?"

Granny flushed.

"Think I'm trusting my granddaughter to some tattooed trucker I don't even know?" she asked. She narrowed her eyes. "Who are your people, son? Where you from?"

The trucker told her. It turned out he had kin in Pine Hollow. He might even have been related to us, in a distant, fourth-cousin-twice-removed kind of way.

"Okay," Granny said finally. "I know who you are. I can trust you."

She walked back to the cab of our truck and started pulling out my suitcase. I panicked.

"Granny!" I whispered behind her. "You're letting me go with him?"

She dropped the suitcase at my feet. She thrust the sleeping bag into my arms.

"He's a Compton," she said. "Everybody knows those Comptons are all too tenderhearted even to swat a fly. You'll be fine."

I looked up and down the deserted road.

"What about you?" I asked.

"Oh, don't worry about me," Granny said. "I'll be up there at Mercer in a week, to pick you up."

The trucker, Granny, and I pushed our truck to the side of the road. Then Granny hugged me goodbye, and I climbed up the tall steps to the semi. The trucker tossed my suitcase and sleeping bag up behind me. He got in and revved the engine. We could still hear Granny yelling after us.

"You take good care of her now, you hear? Remember, I know your people!"

"Is it exciting?" I asked the trucker after we'd gone several miles with nothing between us but the drone of the engine.

"Huh?"

"Is it exciting?" I repeated. "Driving all over the place, seeing all sorts of different places?"

He fixed me with the same kind of look Dad always gives me when I do something particularly dumb.

"All's I ever see is road," he said. "Believe me, if there was a single other job in Spit Creek, Kentucky, that I could support my family on, I'd be doing it."

We drove on in silence for a while. I noticed that he didn't look right or left, didn't lift his eyes from the pavement at all. That's probably what the trucking company wanted him to do, but still. We had passed fields of sunflowers, a whole farm where they grew nothing but grass (the sign said, Let us be your lawn!) and a house with an honest-to-God turret. I'd never seen a turret before in my life.

"You know turtles—box turtles?" the trucker said suddenly, surprising me so much I could barely nod. "Someone takes a turtle away from where it belongs, the turtle will spend its whole life trying to get back home. And turtles live a long time. Fifty years, maybe even a hundred."

"That's a long time to go around feeling homesick," I said.

The trucker nodded, like he thought I understood.

An hour later, the trucker dropped me off in front of Mercer Hall at Mercer University and departed in a belch of smoke. When I watched that big silver semi drive off, I had to blink a couple times to keep myself from thinking it was a turtle shell. Then I turned around and faced Mercer Hall.

"They invited me," I whispered to myself. "They want me here."

Still, I was kind of glad that Granny wasn't standing right there with me. I was glad the trucker had gone away. If there'd been something behind me to go back to, I couldn't have made my feet go forward.

Or—maybe I couldn't make my feet go forward, anyway. I stood there, staring up at the stern brick building, until someone pushed open the door.

"Hey!" a girl yelled. "Are you here for the College for High Schoolers program?"

"Y-yes," I stammered.

"Well, come on in," she said heartily. "You have just enough time to take your luggage to your room before orientation."

That was the push I needed. The girl, who introduced herself as Claire, maneuvered me through a registration form, a trip to a dorm room I'd be sharing with someone else, and a return to Mercer Hall. I stepped into a living room of sorts filled with other kids.

"Hey there, everyone!" Claire announced. "This is Lindley."

"Everyone" turned and looked. I looked back. I felt like I'd stepped onto the set of *Dawson's Creek*. Everyone had beautiful skin, beautiful hair, beautiful teeth. I decided I was thinking too much like my uncle Lester, who's a horse trader and sometimes takes to evaluating humans the same way as animals. I switched my attention to everyone's clothes. The boys were mostly wearing T-shirts and shorts; the girls were wearing skintight tanks or T's and shorts.

I was wearing a dress.

Furthermore, my suitcase back in the dorm room was

full of folded-up dresses, brand-new from Wal-Mart. Oops. Why had I relied on *The Bell Jar* to know what kids wore to college? I should have remembered that Sylvia Plath went to college in the 1950s. Years and years and years ago.

"Where are you from?" the girl in the tightest tank and the skimpiest shorts asked me.

"Oh, I'm an exchange student from Appalachia," I said ruefully.

I felt so out of place in that dress, I was ready to offer up myself and my home for comic relief. As Granny always says, sometimes it pays to laugh at yourself before anyone else has a chance to. But nobody laughed. Looking at the blank look on tight-tank girl's face, I decided *Time* magazine was right, and American teens nowadays were woefully ignorant of geography.

"Well," tight-tank girl said, "you certainly speak English beautifully. There's just a trace of an accent."

I sat down.

Claire started in on the program, telling us what a wonderful week we were going to have. We were all supposed to introduce ourselves and tell what we wanted to major in when we got to college for real. The tight-tank girl's name was Daphne, and she planned to get a doctorate in engineering.

"You?" a haughty boy with dark, curly hair said. He'd introduced himself as "Justin—political science with an economics minor."

Daphne flipped her long blond hair over her shoulder. "Hello?" she said. "I've won the state science fair the past three years. A doctorate in engineering is just the *beginning* of my plans."

That shut Justin up, though as we all learned later, he wasn't one to keep his mouth closed for long.

When it was my turn, I said my name loud and proud, then kind of mumbled, "I don't know what I want to major in." I didn't add, "I probably won't get to go to college for real." Everyone else seemed to be taking it for granted.

"That's okay," Daphne said comfortingly. "You're an exchange student. The university system probably isn't the same in your country."

The others must not have heard what I'd said earlier, because now there was a little flurry of whispers around the circle. I heard, "Oh, an exchange student. That explains it," and "Where's she from?" and an overconfident, too-loud answer from Justin, "I think it's one of those poor, formerly Communist countries in Eastern Europe. See how bad her teeth are?"

I should have corrected them once and for all, said, "Hello? Don't you know that Appalachia starts right at the eastern edge of your state?" But I was too busy trying to make sure my lips hid my bad teeth.

And as the days passed, I discovered it was right handy having everyone think I was a foreigner. Because of that, nobody was surprised that I was the only person who hadn't taken an eighth-grade trip to Washington, D.C., who couldn't brag, as Justin did, "Well, when I saw the Constitution and the Declaration of Independence at the National Archives, I was not impressed. . . ." Nobody minded explaining to me that college cafeterias are in different buildings than the classrooms, not like high school at all. Nobody seemed concerned that I mostly sat silently in the back of the group, just listening.

Still, I decided that thirty-year-old textbooks, the Pine Hollow library, *Time* magazine—and teachers who sometimes slipped and said "ain't" themselves—hadn't given me *that* bad of an education. Once, I was the only person who could name all the Cabinet officials of the current administration, even more than Justin could.

"I got everyone but the Secretary of the Interior," Justin sulked at lunch that day. "It's not my fault that one changed last week. I was at computer camp then."

"You?" Daphne teased. Justin had made it clear all along that he had nothing but contempt for computer experts—or "techno-drones," as he called them.

Justin blushed.

"My dad thinks that's where the money is," he muttered. "He just doesn't take a long-term view. Sure, when I'm president, I won't be making that much—but then there'll be hefty speaking fees for years after that, and fame and honor. . . ."

"'*When* you're president?'" Daphne asked. "When, not *if*?"

"Of course," Justin said. "You're not the only one who's got everything planned."

I thought about my own future plans, which were—nothing. I wasn't even sure I could count on Granny being there at the end of the week to pick me up.

When I tuned back in to the conversation, Justin and Daphne were arguing about the whole point of College for High Schoolers.

"It's such a joke, really," Justin was saying. "We all know it's a marketing ploy on the university's part, to try to get the state's smartest kids to come here, when everyone knows we belong at Harvard or Yale."

"Or M.I.T.," Daphne added.

"Whatever," Justin said. "Do they really think *any* of us would settle for a second-rate institution like this?"

I hadn't known Mercer was second-rate. I'd thought it was world-class. State-of-the-art.

The pizza I was chewing started tasting like cardboard. I swallowed carefully.

"Then why are you here now?" I asked Justin quietly.

He shrugged. "It got me away from my dad for another week," he said.

"And he didn't get into Harvard's summer program," a pimply-faced boy named Ryan said from down the table.

"That's not true!" Justin said, gripping the table like he was ready to spring up and start throwing punches.

"Hey, hey, I was just joking," Ryan said. "Sheesh."

Then the whole tableful of kids began comparing all

the different camps and summer programs they'd gone to in their lives, dating back to first grade. Soccer camp, ballet camp, young inventors' camp, discovery camp, math camp, writers' camp. . . . I got quieter and quieter, and I wondered that nobody else noticed. What was I going to say? *Back in Pine Hollow, we'uns have a summer reading program at the library. Kids go there and the librarian reads them books?* Once upon a time, I'd been mighty impressed with that program.

"Know what I did last month?" Ryan said. "I had work camp with my church youth group. We went to South Carolina and put roofs on poor people's houses."

"Oh, that sounds thrilling," Justin said. I think he was still mad about Ryan's Harvard comment.

"Well, it was kind of interesting," Ryan said. "I want to be a sociologist, you know? And the people down there, you just can't figure them out. They live in these old, falling-down shacks in the mountains—or maybe, maybe, a rusty old trailer—but they've all got these huge satellite dishes and big-screen TVs. Things my dad would say *we* couldn't afford."

"Maybe they just like TV," I said in such a small voice I was surprised anyone else heard me. Or maybe everyone else heard better than I did. My ears had started ringing. I went on. "Maybe they just care more about what their TVs look like than what their houses look like. And in the mountains, maybe they wouldn't get any reception at all without that satellite dish. It's not like there's cable wires strung out everywhere in the country."

Suddenly everyone was staring at me.

"You don't understand," Ryan said. "These people are on *welfare*. They're taking *charity*."

"So they don't have a right to watch *Oprah*?" I said fiercely. "Or soap operas or game shows or Saturday morning cartoons?"

"Ah, a good question has been raised here," Justin interjected, sounding like one of those pompous moderators on political talk shows. "Do Americans have a basic right to TV? Even poor people? Even at taxpayers' expense?"

"It's not at taxpayers' expense," I said. "Welfare doesn't pay for televisions."

"But if these people can't afford to feed their families, how can they afford TVs? Top-of-the-line, big-screen TVs?" Ryan asked.

"They work for them," I said. "They work *hard*." My eyes blurred then, to go along with my ringing ears. I was going to cry. I shoved myself away from the table and ran away. Tears began dripping down my face before I even passed the serving line.

One of the cooks saw me and called out, "Are you all right, honey?" I shrugged and kept going, though the cook probably would have understood better than the whole cafeteria full of smart-alecky, know-it-all, too-big-for-their-pants rich kids. I ducked out a side door, into a clump of trees. Hidden by a huge shrub, I crouched down and let myself sob.

If I hadn't started crying, I could have flung all sorts of arguments out at Ryan. *My mother's been working at McDonald's for twenty years, and she still makes the same as me: minimum wage. You want to tell me we don't deserve food stamps? Ever been in a coal mine? That's where my granddad worked. Days went by when he never saw the sun. And then he died of the black lung. And my granny? Want to know why she had to drop out of school? Eleven years old, she had to go to work in a tomato-canning factory to support her family.* But no—I couldn't have said any of that without exposing myself, exposing my family.

The shrubbery around me started moving, and the next thing I knew, Justin and Daphne were peeking through the leaves at me.

"Go away," I growled.

"We just wanted to—" Daphne began.

"Apologize," Justin finished. "That Ryan can be such a jerk."

That struck me as truly ridiculous—like the pot calling the kettle a little shady.

"It was just an academic discussion," Justin said. "Nothing personal."

"I live in a trailer," I said. "We have a satellite dish. And a big-screen TV."

"Oh," Daphne said weakly. "But in your country, probably—"

"Look at a map," I said. "Appalachia's part of Ohio."

They both blinked at me a few times. Then Justin said, "I knew that. I just thought you said you were from somewhere else."

I gave him such a scornful look he actually took a step backward.

"I don't belong here," I said. "I just want to go home. And you know what's really stupid? I can't. Any of the rest of you, you could just call Mommy or Daddy, and they'd be right here, 'Was that big bad university mean to my little sweet-ums?' Not me. I'm stuck here the rest of the week, everybody thinking . . . everybody knowing . . ."

"Doesn't your family have a phone?" Daphne said gently.

"Of course we have a phone," I snarled. Explaining about Granny's truck, everyone else's immobility, was too complicated. I just repeated, "I don't belong here. I shouldn't have come."

I pushed past them in search of a better place to hide.

By dinnertime I'd resorted to hiding out in my room, lying facedown on my bed. I'd skipped all the afternoon sessions, and I'd pretended to be asleep when my roommate tiptoed in to dump her books before dinner.

"I think she's sick," I heard her report to someone in the hall as she slipped back out.

Good, I thought. *Maybe they'll feel sorry for me now.*

But wasn't that the point—that I didn't want anyone feeling sorry for me? To be honest, I was starting to feel a little foolish. Did I really think I was going to lie here on this bed for the next four days? I was already getting bored.

Someone knocked on my door.

"Lindley?" It was Daphne. "I know you're in there. I have something to show you. I'll slide it under the door."

I wanted to keep lying there, stubborn and still, but my curiosity got the better of me. Very quietly, I got up and inched over to the door.

A thin square of paper was on the floor, half in my room, half out. Maybe Daphne hadn't fully made up her mind that she wanted me to see it. I picked it up. It was a picture—a school picture of a girl with painful-looking braces and glasses as thick as canning jars and stringy hair the color of a grocery sack.

"That's me," Daphne said from the other side of the door.

"No way," I said aloud.

"Yes it is," Daphne said. "Open the door and you'll see."

I opened the door and there was Daphne, looking as much like an MTV Spring Break contestant as ever. Justin was standing right behind her.

"That's how I looked until a month ago," Daphne said. "So now you know a secret about me, too. I brought that picture with me—I don't know, just to remind myself."

I looked again, back and forth between the picture and Daphne. There was something familiar about the cheekbones of the girl in the picture. Still, I couldn't make my eyes see her as Daphne.

"So?" I said rudely. "You're blond and beautiful now."

"And you know what? I'm not sure I like it," Daphne said. She glanced back at Justin, but he didn't say anything. She kept talking. "I don't like people expecting me to be dumb. When I was ditsy before, it was like, 'Oh, absent-minded genius. Einstein never learned how to tie his shoes either.' Now it's, 'Dumb blond. Of course.' It's awful. I probably couldn't even win a local science fair looking like this."

"Oh," I said weakly.

Daphne nudged Justin in the ribs. "Your turn," she said.

Justin looked jolted, like he'd just intended to come along as an observer.

"For what?" he said.

"To tell us a secret," Daphne said. "So we'll all be even."

I thought he was going to refuse—probably on the grounds that it might hurt his future presidential campaign. But he took a deep breath and said, rapid-fire, "I really didn't get into the Harvard summer program. And my dad said it didn't matter, because I don't have the social skills to be a politician, anyway. That's the real reason he wants me to go into computers."

"Your own father said that? Ouch," I said.

"See? None of the rest of us know who we are either," Daphne said.

I leaned against the doorway. Maybe I should have let her comment go, accepted the secrets she and Justin were telling me, and pretended to get along for the rest of the week. But I couldn't.

"You don't understand," I said. "I *do* know who I am. That's the problem. I'm bologna on white bread. Casseroles made with Velveeta. Old cars rusting up on cinder blocks for decades on end. Nasty old shacks with satellite dishes behind them. I'm not—my people aren't—we're not *college material.*"

Daphne seemed to be trying very hard to accept that people actually ate Velveeta. I looked over at Justin, expecting to see him trying out a (failed) politician's smile. But he was shaking his head.

"Maybe you are all that," he said. "But you're also one of us. You do belong here. Think about it. You *memorized* all the Cabinet positions."

"Dating back five administrations," I said shakily.

"Really?" Justin said. "I only know four."

"I was scared there'd be a test," I admitted.

"Glory be," Daphne said, in an imitation of what she probably thought was an Appalachian accent. "You're an even bigger geek than the rest of us!"

Granny showed up at the end of the week, just like she'd promised. The truck's engine was positively purring. And she wasn't alone.

"This here's Earl," she said, pointing to the stout, muscular man who got out of the truck with her. "He was the mechanic in Spindler."

"So you've been in Spindler all week?" I asked.

She glanced back at Earl. Maybe it was just the sunlight, but I think she might have been blushing.

"No, no, child," she said. "We've been visiting around all over the place. Travel is so . . . enlightening. Earl wanted me to meet all his kin. Soon as we drop you off in Pine Hollow, we're going to go meet the rest of them."

She smiled up at Earl, who smiled back at her. I had a feeling my circle of relatives was about to grow.

"Ready?" Earl said, effortlessly lifting my suitcase into the bed of the truck.

"In a minute," I said. I gave Mercer one last look around. Justin was getting into a silver Saab. Daphne was climbing into a blue minivan that seemed to be filled with younger girls in varying sizes, all wearing glasses. I noticed that Daphne was wearing glasses now, too. I felt like I was seeing the beginnings of a makeover in reverse. Several other kids were staring at Granny and Earl and me. And the truck. I just smiled and waved and held my shoulders high. Then I slipped onto the seat beside Granny.

"So. You get your fill of college?" Earl asked as we drove down the street, lofty academic buildings whizzing past.

"No," I said. "I think I'll probably be back next year. In the fall. To stay for good."

Granny kind of gasped, and Earl said, "What for?"

I just shrugged. "Why not?" I said. There were too many answers to go into. *Because Justin and Daphne are seriously considering Mercer now, too . . . Because Claire says I have a good shot at a full scholarship . . . Because I belong at Mercer as much as I belong in Pine Hollow . . . Because now I know who my people are. The rest of them.*

I wasn't sure how that was going to work, me being two different kinds of people at the same time. Would I start eating Belgian endive on my bologna sandwiches? Would I write papers quoting Dolly Parton and Plato in alternate sentences?

I didn't care. I'd been somewhere now. And it didn't look like there were any limits at all anymore on where else I could go.

☀

ABOUT THE AUTHOR

Everyone likes to travel in Margaret Peterson Haddix's family. Her husband jokes that if someone asks, "Do you want to go?" they all say, "Sure!" before they even know where they're agreeing to go. Margaret Peterson Haddix is thus greatly intrigued whenever she meets people who literally have never been outside their hometowns. She says, "I'm always desperately trying to find a polite way to ask, 'Don't you ever wonder what's on the other side of that mountain? Or across the next state line?'" And so she created Lindley, a teenager who understands her family's way of life but isn't sure of her own curiosity and wanderlust. Her journey to Mercer University is life-changing.

Although Margaret Peterson Haddix travels with her family whenever she can, she mostly sits at her desk in her Ohio home, writing award-winning novels for young people on a wide variety of topics. She has published a time-travel novel *(Running Out of Time)*, three futuristic novels *(Among the Hidden, Among the Imposters,* and *Turnabout)*, a realistic novel about parental abandonment and abuse *(Don't You Dare Read This, Mrs. Dunphrey)*, another about religious extremists *(Leaving Fishers)*, and a novel about what happens to Cinderella after she is found by Prince Charming *(Just Ella)*. Almost all of her novels have been designated Best Books for Young Adults by the American Library Association, and four of them have been Quick Picks, with *Among the Hidden* voted one of the Top 10 Best Books of the year and one of the Top 10 Quick Picks as well. Her newest novel, *Takeoffs and Landings,* is also about a life-changing journey.

From his family of thieves and con artists, Jared has learned well.
But does he have the patience as well as the talent to make the
big score from the old lady who lives alone at the edge of town?

Bad Blood

Will Weaver

I knocked on the door.

Waited.

Inside the farmhouse I heard a radio go quiet, then shuffling sounds. I had a good feeling about this place; it was set well off the road, and the old lady appeared to live alone.

She opened the door partway. "Yes?" Her voice was thin and croaky from lack of use.

"Good morning, ma'am," I chirped. "My name's Jared Righetti and I'm looking for summer work. Painting, lawn mowing, odd jobs?" One good thing about being an undersized sixteen-year-old is that I can pass for thirteen. I tried to see beyond her, into the house.

"No, nothing for you," she said, and stepped back from the screen door. The shades were half-drawn — what is it with old people and daylight? — so I couldn't see much. However, it smelled like an old person's house — stale, fruity, soggy tea bags, flowers, cats, all of it mixed together like the odor of old carpet.

"Okay, ma'am," I said. I flashed her my winning smile (learned from my old man). "Sorry to bother you." I headed down her porch steps and pedaled off with my lawn mower in tow — except that I went only a short way before turning back.

"What is it now?" she said. She was still at the screen door. "I told you I have no work for you."

"I understand, ma'am," I said. "But I'm in the Boy Scouts, and we get pins for doing volunteer work. I'm wondering if you'd mind if I mowed your lawn for free? It won't take me long. It's part of the Boy Scout oath — to do volunteer work."

She was silent, then cleared her throat with a raspy sound. "Okay. But just that front part."

"Thank you, ma'am!" I said, and saluted.

Boy Scouts. Ha.

As I started up my mower, I felt her gaze on me. When I began to move back and forth across the shaggy lawn, her white head peeped from behind the window. Her fuzzy white hair looked like the dandelion seed globes that my mower scattered in the wind.

I had spotted this place when my family first landed in this lame, white-bread Ohio town. I almost said Iowa; we've moved around so much, sometimes I forget where we are. Anyway, I was riding my bike, casing the town— which I had to admit looked perfect for us. My father was a genius in choosing places such as Oakville, population 7,500. Here people left their car windows open, left their garage doors up in the daytime, and left their kids' bikes lying on lawns. It was one of those little towns that the real world hadn't caught up to yet—a petty thief's dream.

Trouble was, my father had drummed into me that we were not petty thieves. Thieves, all right, but not smalltimers. "The dollar bill is lying on the table, and all you have to do is reach over and pick it up. But it's not the dollar you want, or the ten-spot, or even the whole wallet. Set your sights higher, son." But stealing was in my blood. I didn't see a woman shopping; I saw her purse loosely slung over her shoulder. I didn't see a man walking down the street; I saw his wallet peeking from his hip pocket. I didn't see a photographer shooting a sundown scene; I saw his camera bag unattended. It was genetic.

Anyway, back to the old lady. That first week here I had ridden all the way to the city limits and a little beyond—which was scary. All that open space, all those cornfields with tall, tight, shadowy rows. My parents had warned me about Midwestern cornfields, about kids getting lost in them and never found. Big fields and open horizons gave me the creeps—give me honking taxis and narrow streets any day (also probably genetic). So just as I was about to pedal like mad back to town, I saw a narrow driveway, and beyond—back off the road at least a block—an old white farmhouse. Saggy barn. Tall hay shed, along with various cribs and coops. And a lawn in major need of mowing. Elmer A. Anderson, the mailbox read.

Even as I looked, a little white-haired lady shuffled onto her porch to water some red flowers in a window box. I sank low in the ditch so she wouldn't see me and I watched her for quite a while. I got the feeling there was no Elmer around. At age sixteen I already had a nose for lonely old widows; sometimes I amazed and disgusted myself at the same time.

Today when I finished mowing, I rattled my mower back to my bike. On Mrs. Anderson's porch steps sat a tall glass of iced tea. "I wouldn't feel right without giving you something for your trouble," she said from behind the screen.

"Whew! It's hot—thank you so much, Mrs. Anderson," I exclaimed.

"How'd you know my name?" she said suspiciously.

"The mailbox?" I answered.

She was silent.

I took my time with the iced tea, but finally finished the last, long, cold swallow. I approached the screen door with the empty glass.

"Just set it on the porch," she said.

"Thank you. Bye, Mrs. Anderson," I called cheerfully over my shoulder. Through her watery little eyes I imagined seeing myself: a smallish brown-haired kid on his bike, heading down the driveway towing his lawn mower on a rope. The image should be a Norman Rockwell painting. *Summer Job* would be the title. That or *Honest Hardworking Young Man.*

However, as far as I could see, there hadn't been any honest, hard-working men in my family for generations. My great-grandfather, whose last name was unpronounceable (it had several Z's and Y's), was some kind of King of the Gypsies back in immigrant days in New York City. His pickpocketing skills bordered on magic and the dark arts. People not only didn't miss their wallets or coin purses; they forgot they ever had them. (My father knows the moves but won't teach them to me—his own son. "They'll just get you in trouble, and besides, son, you've got to set your sights high in this world." If I hear that one more time, I swear I'll become an actual nice honest young man just to punish him.) My grandfather, Alphonse Szymoro, founded the so-called Travelers, the world's largest fly-by-night roofing and home repair company. It's based in Skokie, Illinois. Don't believe me? *Sixty Minutes* did an investigative report on the Travelers but all CBS got were some blurry long-distance photos of white Ford F-150 pickup trucks carrying ladders and cans of roofing tar. Most of the segment was interviews with geezers all weepy about paying thousands of dollars for roof repairs and still needing rain buckets in their living rooms. When Mike Wallace began to talk about money—how the Travelers wives all drove Cadillacs—my mother gave my old man the evil eye. "Always I said we should have stayed with the family," she said. (Her family was Eastern European as well—thick as thieves, you might say.)

"Nonsense," my father said. He was a tidy, dark-haired man with brown eyes and an open, likable face and a sense of humor that tended to one-liners. His favorite: "America's biggest problem is that it's overrun with private property." (It is sort of funny, considering.) Anyway, now he continued, "You don't see *Sixty Minutes* peeking in our windows, do you? The bigger you get, the bigger target you make. The three of us—we're on nobody's radar, and every penny we make, we keep."

"Right," I muttered sarcastically. I happened to know that my old man had been drummed out of the larger clan for cheating them. In other words, not only was my father a crook, he was a dishonest crook. But he was a great father. Hey—you can't have everything.

My mother had nothing more to say about her imaginary Cadillac, because in many ways my old man was right. Here we were in a nice rented home, a three-bedroom rambler, with a green lawn and bright flower beds.

We had settled quietly into this neighborhood, and now were just another family on East Maple Drive. Okay, slightly darker skinned, and brown-eyed rather than blue, and a foot shorter than most of the corn-fed Swedish and German stock around here. But we passed for Italian (Righetti was my favorite name so far), and Italians get a pass in the Midwest because they are associated with Italian restaurants. Nobody eats more than Midwesterners; it's why they're so fat.

Anyway, there was always the question of jobs — how my family supported itself — but as usual my father had that covered. My mother was an interior decorator (the perfect job for casing houses) and my father was a wholesaler involved in supplying olive oil to Italian pizza joints across the Midwest. I didn't know exactly what scam he had going right now, but he was very cheerful of late, and I got the feeling he was closing in on something big.

But then again, so was I.

The next part I'll skip through, because it's as boring as a public television documentary on life in the Midwest. See me mowing Mrs. Anderson's lawn, front and back, the next time. See me returning once a week to Mrs. Anderson's farm. See me trimming the hedge. See me painting the porch railing. See me trying to get a look into the outbuildings, but see her always watching me from her chair on the porch. See me raking her leaves in the fall. See me shoveling snow in the winter. See me working in her garden the next spring. See me waiting for my chance—at what I didn't know. See me inside her gloomy house, having my snack, politely munching a sugar cookie and sipping my iced tea. See me checking drawers in the kitchen, desks in the living room the first time she left me alone. See me notice, one day, through the parlor doors (never opened quite this far) a photo display on the wall—like a shrine in a church—except this was a shrine to a soldier.

"That man on the wall, is that your husband?"

Mrs. Anderson stiffened. "No," she said abruptly, and hurried to shut the parlor door.

Next week when I arrived to work, I knocked and knocked. It wasn't locked, so I stepped inside. Mrs. Anderson was in the parlor, just sitting, staring at the soldier on the wall. It's like she hadn't moved for an entire week.

"Hello? It's me, Jared," I called.

She turned slowly; it was as if she didn't recognize me.

"I'm going to start on the garage today," I said cheerfully. "Scraping and painting."

"It's his birthday," she murmured.

I stepped forward to the parlor entrance. For the first time I got a good look around. It was like a museum filled with antiques—valuable antiques.

"His birthday?" I said.

"Garry," she said to the wall. Creepylike, as if she was talking to Garry.

I looked closer at the shrine. There were several photos of Garry, one with helicopters and a jungle in the background.

"Garry, my son," she murmured, as if calling out to him.

There was a framed and yellowed newspaper clipping. "Local Marine Garrett Anderson Killed in Vietnam." The date was July 16, 1969. I got it: her dead son.

"He would be fifty today," she whispered. "Fifty years old. Isn't that amazing."

"Yes, it is," I agreed as I made a note of the antiques: some great old lamps, a lion's head rocking chair, an actual wind-up Victrola phonograph, plus an eight-track tape deck and a shelf of clunky, oversized eight-track tapes: Bob Dylan; Crosby, Stills, Nash and Young; the Byrds; others with faded daisylike and psychedelic designs. Eight-tracks were worth a lot of money nowadays; people collected them.

Mrs. Anderson blinked; she seemed surprised to see me standing there. "I'm starting on the garage today," I said again. Loudly, cheerfully. As always.

She didn't seem to hear me and turned back to look at the soldier on the wall. Which gave me the opportunity—at last—to case the outbuildings without her spying on me.

The garage was gloomy and full of spiders. It looked like a museum of rusty tools and shovels, not a hundred bucks' worth of goods. So I slipped over into the barn.

The door creaked and pigeons clattered out of the hayloft. My heart pounded; the damned birds scared me. It took a while for my eyes to adjust to the light, which revealed a long row of rusty stanchions and a few old shovels and forks lying here and there. Zilch. Zero.

Coming out of the barn, I looked around. The only other building was a hay shed: a metal roof supported by tall poles, and open sides. I still don't know why I walked over to it, and certainly can't explain why I walked around back, behind it. The thief in me, I guess.

A few bales had sagged and spilled out to the ground. They were black and rotted. I kicked at them. Just as I was about to give up on finding anything of value, I spotted a different kind of green in the haystack. Some kind of canvas or tarpaulin. I tugged loose a couple of bales and looked closer. The canvas, mouse-chewn so badly it looked shot by a machine gun, was draped over some kind of wooden frame. Beams, heavy ones. Some kind of secret garage.

I got down and dug out some bottom bales until I could slip underneath the canvas. Inside the canvas enclosure it was dark except for the bullet holes. Standing up, I hit my head on something hard; suddenly I had plenty of light—as in stars—little arcing pinwheels of white.

To steady myself I reached out and felt curving metal sticky with some kind of grease. "Ack," I muttered, and wiped my hand on the scratchy hay.

I needed more light so crawled backward out of there and began to remove more bales. Soon I had a double doorway–sized area clear, and found a corner of the canvas. It was nailed to the wooden frame. I glanced around; seeing or hearing no one, I yanked it upward.

With a ripping sound, the canvas came loose; light spilled into the secret garage. Inside was a car.

A small car covered in grease.

A small, squat car with lines and curves that anyone would instantly recognize: an old Corvette.

I sucked in a breath. It's not the dollar bill or the ten-spot or even the whole wallet! Peeking around the hay shed toward the house, and seeing nothing of old lady Anderson, I stepped inside the secret garage and tried the car door. Grease, everything coated with grease, as if painted or broomed on, but the door opened. The little cockpit sat empty, its stick shift with its little round knob sticking upright between the seats. I slid over behind the wheel, and my hand fell immediately to the stick shift; the car fit me like a glove. I wiped dust from the dashboard, the gauges. The odometer read 562 miles. The *bumpa-bumpa* of my heart echoed louder inside the dim cab. A classic Corvette with less than a thousand miles on it. The car had to be worth twenty or thirty grand.

In the glove box were some papers. A faded green title sheet with all the information. Make: Chev. Year: 1964. Model: Coupé (Stingray). Owner: Garrett Elmer

Anderson. One other paper, a yellow sheet of tablet paper, fell out of the title papers.

Dear Mom and Dad,

Take care of my 'Ray. When we win this war, which shouldn't take long, I'll come home and I'll drive you down Main Street in the Fourth of July parade.

I promise.

Love, Garry

The rest of that afternoon I loudly and cheerfully scraped window trim on the garage. I whistled while I worked, and kept one eye on the house. Finally the old lady came out on the porch. She seemed older in just two hours and walked bent over as if she carried a hundred pounds on her bony shoulders.

I thought she'd never bring out an iced tea, but finally she remembered. I joined her on the porch. We sat there in silence.

"Hot one today," I said. "Whew."

She was silent.

"But I'm happy for the work," I said.

She stared off across the fields. Her eyes were cloudy today.

"I'm saving my money for college, you know."

She had nothing to say.

I took a deep breath. "That and a car."

No response.

"If I had a car, I could drive out here anytime you needed me," I added.

She blinked, seemed to consider that. "Garry had an old car," she murmured, still looking across the fields. "Funny little thing, it was. He worked summers at the gas station to buy that car. Was so proud of it."

Then I took a chance, a big chance. "There's a little old car in the hay shed," I said. "Would that be it?"

"Car in the hay shed?" she repeated. "You mean a tractor?"

"No, a little old car," I replied as if I was uninterested — as if this was the most boring topic in the world.

"I don't know what Garry did with his little car," she murmured. "So hard to remember everything."

"Just a little old car in the hay shed," I drawled and pretended to check some paint chips under my fingernails.

She looked through the parlor at the soldier on the wall, then around her house. "I hardly drive my Pontiac anymore," she said. "I certainly don't need two cars."

I felt shaky; things were happening fast; things were coming together. It was a major adrenaline rush — and I suddenly understood why the men in my family could never hold straight jobs.

"Why don't you take it, Jared?" she said.

"The little car in the hay shed?" I asked. My voice was suddenly as thin and shaky as hers.

"Why would I need two cars? I hardly drive the Pontiac anymore."

I swallowed, then took a gamble. "No, Mrs. Anderson, I couldn't do that. You've been awfully nice to me too, and while the car probably isn't worth much, I just couldn't accept a gift like that."

"Why, you're always helping out around here," she continued, like she hadn't heard me. She actually came over and patted me on the head—it was the first time we had touched. "This place would have fallen down without you. Such a nice young fellow. I think you should take it. Why would I need two cars? I hardly drive the Pontiac anymore."

"I'll . . . think about it," I said. I was so excited that I almost tipped my glass. "Right now I'd better get back to work."

"I hardly drive the Pontiac anymore," she murmured as I left.

Outside, I let out a deep breath. I hurried back into the secret garage and examined the title page again: it was clear that if I could get her signature in a couple of places, the Corvette was mine. I couldn't believe my luck. I did a crazy little victory dance—wait till my old man saw this car.

Then I heard a sound and peeked back around the hay shed; I saw her shuffling across her porch, so I stuffed the title papers inside my shirt and resumed work on the garage. I watched her lift a watering can to her petunias.

Her arms shook so badly that she spilled most of the water. I turned away—I couldn't watch.

That night, at home, my father asked, "So how's the old lady?" He had come to be a little puzzled at my loyalty to Mrs. Anderson. I think he worried that I was turning into a nice young honest fellow.

"Better and better," I said, trying to sound sly. In truth I had this weird mix of emotions swirling in my head.

"Great," my father answered. He flashed a white-toothed smile (sometimes I swear he could pass for Omar Sharif and be in the movies). "Anything you'll need help with?"

"If I do, I'll let you know." I was suddenly crabby.

He nodded. "Remember, son—" he began.

"I know, I know. Nothing illegal, nothing I can't walk away from, don't get greedy, blah blah." I'd heard all that one too many times.

"That's right," he said gently. "Good luck."

I shrugged. It was difficult to stay angry at him. "Anyway, it's in the bag," I said.

He patted me on the head. "I'm proud of you, son."

Later, in bed, I lay in the dark with my eyes closed. I saw myself cruising in Garry Anderson's Corvette. At first it was just me, then me and a girl—a blond college coed. Then I must have drifted off, because I was in college, studying to be a doctor or an astronaut—something all-American—and it was clear that the blond girl and I would be married and have two perfect children, and I would take my family for Sunday afternoon drives in the Corvette, and when we passed, people would look up and remark, "Such a nice family."

The next night I had another Corvette dream. It started out with the blond girl again, but then it was me at the wheel, and Mr. and Mrs. Anderson were in the back seat. People were gathering for a parade. Firecrackers and fireworks kept going off, in loud booms and sharp machine-gun-like rattles, and then the parade began. It was the Fourth of July, and I was driving proudly down the street, wearing a Boy Scout's uniform and saluting all the people waving and clapping—except in the crowd I kept seeing flashes of this ragged-looking soldier. He was burned or injured somehow, and he just kept staring at me. From this dream I woke up with a start; my heart was pounding.

The third night I had a dream that made no sense. I was in this health club, in the weight room with all these bodybuilders. Me, an undersized, pencil-necked sixteen-year-old who couldn't lift one of the massive iron plates they were pumping. I watched them in awe (me watching would have made yet another Norman Rockwell painting). Then I went up to the biggest guy and in a cheerful, totally optimistic voice said, "Excuse me, sir. I want to change how I look. If I start lifting weights today, how long do you think it would take for me to look like you?"

The buffalo-necked guy glared down at me, then lifted me by my neck with one hand and examined my scrawny body. "How long would it take for you to look like me? I'd say at least three to four generations." Everyone in the club laughed wildly.

The next day I felt hyper, felt shaky—like today was the day it had to be done. Now or never. Fish or cut bait.

I biked out to Mrs. Anderson's right away in the morning. She looked like she had been wearing the same dress all week. She didn't even get out of her chair when I came in.

"Garry!" she said.

"No, Jared," I said loudly.

She blinked; then her eyes filled with water. "I'm sorry, Jared. Don't know what I was thinking."

"It's okay," I said quickly. I drew up a chair and produced the title sheet to the Corvette. "I've changed my mind; I'd like to have the little car in the hay shed," I said.

She stared at me.

"The one you offered to me," I added.

"That would be fine," she murmured. "I don't even drive my Pontiac anymore."

"You'll have to sign on the title page," I said clearly and loudly. "Do you understand?" *Nothing illegal, nothing you can't walk away from . . .*

"Yes, I understand," she said.

I had a pen ready. If I hadn't, if one thing had gone wrong—say the pen ran dry—I swear I would have bolted.

But I didn't.

"There," she said. Her handwriting was crampy but legible.

"And date it," I said. I wanted everything in her handwriting, everything legal.

"What is the date?" she asked.

I told her the day and year.

She looked up quickly. "How is that possible?" she murmured. "That means Garry is fifty."

"Right there," I said, pointing to the line. "Fill in the date right there." My voice was high and faster now. I was sweating. Images of my dream Fourth of July parade filled my head. Garry on the wall stared down at me. I thought I might throw up.

But then it was done. "Thank you so much," I said. I touched her bony hand—it was cool, almost cold. I drew back, then hurried toward the door.

"Jared?" she called after me. "Garry?"

Mrs. Anderson croaked only two weeks later. I was the one who found her, which I prefer not to talk about, other than that she was on the kitchen floor. Her false teeth had come out, and the place didn't smell so good. I guess I knew she was going to tip over sooner rather than later, so to be honest it wasn't a surprise.

Looking back, I could have taken advantage of the moment and cased the entire house—maybe she had money under the mattress—but that would have been a mistake. "Never get greedy," my father always said. "It only calls attention to yourself."

So I called 911, did all the right things. Me, the yard boy who had worked for Mrs. Anderson for nearly two years—loyal to the end. Even some of the distant neighbors, who I didn't know had been watching, knew of my work for her. "More than work, a relationship with Mrs. Anderson," as the attorney for the estate described it. He and the neighbors supported me when some long-lost Andersons appeared at the funeral (which I attended along with my mother and father) and then stayed in town for the reading of the will.

"It always happens," the attorney muttered to me. "Somebody dies all alone, and then the relatives come out of the woodwork." There were objections to the signatures and dates on the Corvette title, but in the end it was no contest—and anyway, the distant relatives ended up with the farm, which they immediately put up for sale.

My father was beside himself with pride. "You've got a great future, son," he kept saying as we loaded the Corvette onto the trailer. "This was masterful. Couldn't have done better myself. And being there at the funeral— what a great touch."

"Thanks," I muttered.

He was so happy he didn't hear me.

As we drove out of the driveway, I looked back at the old white house, at the sagging, shabby buildings, at the dead flowers on the porch. Then we headed onto the highway and picked up speed. As we passed the endless rows of corn, for an instant I thought I saw bony, tattered arms reaching out at me, but they were only corn leaves fluttering in the wind.

My father began to whistle as he drove. I turned to look at him. My father the crook. My grandfather and great-grandfather, all crooks. *At least three to four generations,* the bodybuilder said. I looked behind at the little car on the trailer.

"So, I've found this dealer in Wisconsin who specializes in muscle cars. He'll give top dollar," my father began.

I cut him off. "We'll see," I answered.

He looked at me, surprised.

"Hey, it's my car," I said. "Has my name on the title, if you recall. Which means I can do with it what I want."

His face turned dark with anger, then a moment later opened in a great laugh. "Okay, I get it. Chip off the old block, yes? Just like your old man?"

"Maybe," I said. I looked down the highway ahead of me. "Then again, maybe not."

ABOUT THE AUTHOR

Growing up on a farm in Minnesota, Will Weaver experienced the hardships and pleasures of rural life that have since worked their way into his novels for teenagers as well as adults. His first three young adult novels—*Striking Out, Farm Team,* and *Hard*

Ball—focus on Billy Baggs, a farm boy with an unusually good pitching arm and an overbearing father. All three books were American Library Association Best Books for Young Adults as well as New York Public Library Books for the Teen Age.

More recently, Will Weaver has explored new literary territory in a futuristic novel called *Memory Boy*, a story about how a suburban Minneapolis family copes with adversity after volcanic explosions on the West Coast send showers of ash across the country, bringing normal transportation and city life to a halt. When the book's teenage narrator and his family seek a better life in the countryside, they learn that no place is safe.

When asked where the idea for "Bad Blood" came from, Mr. Weaver says that "the 'found' muscle car story is mythic among motorheads. It's every car guy's dream—to find a rust-free, low-mileage, vintage GTO, Mustang, Chevy, etc." But, of course, his protagonist is not your typical male teenager.

Will Weaver enjoys the short story form so much that he is currently working on a collection of new stories for teens, while continuing to teach English and creative writing at Bemidji State University. You can learn more about him and his publications at www.intraart.com/willweaver.

Because of her irresponsible behavior, Samantha is being forced
by her family to work at a summer camp for underprivileged
kids. If that isn't bad enough, she first has to spend hours
driving there in an old pickup with a geeky kid with
whom she has nothing in common.

Keep Smiling

Alex Flinn

Rachel's friends have been busy. Bouquets of flowers,
mostly dead, are nailed to the tree where she died. Dolls
hang in effigy. Dead candles litter the ground. Notes, written on the wood in marker, cover nearly every inch of the
ficus's gnarled trunk. KEEP SMILING, RACHEL, shouts one.

Dad and I are stuck there, behind a truck full of yard
clippings, on the way to Ian Myers's house. Probably, this
will be the last time I'll see this particular roadside
memorial. When I return after three months as a camp
counselor, Rachel's friends will have moved on with their

lives, found something else to do besides memorializing a girl my age killed by a drunk driver.

I press my face against the windshield.

Dad's talking, but I can barely hear. "There've been problems before this, Samantha—the drinking, your choice of friends. But now . . ." In the reflection, I see him looking past me, at Rachel's memorial. Then he turns away. "I'm hoping that working with people less fortunate than you've been will be a learning experience."

I see a face in the windshield. Is that me? It's like someone I don't know. I stare at it a minute. Then I look through it and meet the blue eyes in Rachel's picture, her senior portrait in cap and gown, tacked to the tree. She never got to graduate. Under the photograph, four pinwheels spin. The breeze from passing cars brings them to life, rolling first one way, then the other with each changing wind.

Keep smiling.

Dad's still talking. Finally, the traffic moves, and we pull away. I can still see Rachel's face, even after we're gone.

"Luck" being a relative term, I guess I'm lucky that Ian Myers lives nearby and is driving up to Camp Seminole, a charity camp for underprivileged kids. Otherwise, it would be Dad and me, all the way from Miami to Podunkville, North Florida (which I'm pretty sure is the town's official name). Six hours.

But that would have given me six hours to talk him out of making me go there.

The first thing I notice at Ian's house is the car. Actually, an old pickup, black, with a camper top that makes it look like a hearse. To complete the image, UNDERTAKERS is painted across the back.

"Come on." Dad's already out, holding my duffel. I stumble out and take the bag, looking at Dad a second to make sure I'm not imagining things. He's really going to make me get into this car and drive away. Finally, I start toward the door.

Dad doesn't walk with me. He just stays by his car, watching.

The guy who answers the door—Ian—is about my age. I don't have to ask whether that's his car. It matches him. Skinny, with longish, dyed-black hair, black army boots, black T-shirt, and baggy shorts, all emphasizing pasty skin. "Oh, boy." He blinks his blue eyes like a creature released from a dark cage.

I remind myself to smile. "What's that supposed to mean?" I say.

He shakes his head. "Just, you don't look much like a camp counselor, Princess."

If you only knew. But I roll my eyes and say, "Well, neither do you." He looks too wimpy to paddle a canoe or anything. I glance back at Dad. Still by the car.

"So they tell me," Ian says. "Whoever *they* are." He

seems to take it as a compliment. It wasn't. Why was I insulted by what he said? Why do I even care?

At school, when people called my friends and me princesses, we weren't offended. We were the reigning monarchs of the school. That's what Ian Myers sees, hair with just the right streaking, my diamond studs, my makeup, my clothes. . . .

But I don't feel like a princess as I step toward Ian's truck. He opens the tailgate. "This your bag?"

"Yeah." It takes me a millisecond to figure out he's not going to lift it. I reach down and heft it on top of his stuff, which takes up about all the space in the truck bed. I look at Dad again, still not believing he's going to make me get into the hearse with Goth boy. But I'm not going to cry or beg him not to make me go. I should go.

Nothing.

I get into the truck, slam the door, and lean against the passenger window.

Ian gets in too. He glances at Dad's car, then at me. He starts to say something but stops. Stops because, at the last possible second, Dad walks over. I open my door thinking, hoping, he won't make me go after all, that somehow things can be like before. But he says, "Be good." When I nod, he goes back to the car and starts the motor.

Ian watches him. Again, he looks like he's thinking about saying something, but he doesn't. Just pulls out the driveway and heads for I-95.

Keep smiling. I face forward. I don't feel like talking. I guess Ian doesn't either. He stares at the road, concentrating too much on his driving. We drive in silence, onto the on ramp, past downtown Miami. It's not long before I can't take the silence anymore. It's too much like the silence in my house. And the silence in my head.

"What is all that stuff?" I gesture toward the crap in the truck bed.

"Music equipment," he says. "Like amps and stuff."

"Are you a music counselor?"

Ian rolls his eyes. "No way. The camp director, she's not into my kind of music. But she said I could practice nights if I didn't bother anyone. I have a band with some guys I know."

A band. How teenage. But I don't say it. Instead I say, "What kind of music do you play?"

This causes Ian to bubble and blurp, turning into a fountain of information. He explains that The Undertakers is his band. He sings and plays lead guitar—heavy metal, none of that mainstream club shit, but a new sound. "We have a demo tape," he says, probably only just noticing my status as captive audience. "Want to hear?"

"Sure." Keep smiling. "Love to." It can't get much worse.

He rummages first in the glove compartment, then under the seat. When he starts to reach around behind the seat, I say, "No. Don't do that. It's dangerous."

He looks up, startled. There's something so familiar about his eyes.

"You should watch the road," I say. "You could have an accident that way."

He nods. "You're right." He turns back frontward.

I reach behind his seat and find the cassette. I stick it into the player.

Music fills the air. To my surprise, it's not terrible. His voice is okay—good, even—and the song isn't bad. "Did you write this?" I ask.

He shakes his head. "My friend John wrote it." The song ends, and Ian meets my eyes. "I wrote this next one."

The music starts up again. This one is even better. Dangerous music—guitars like the wind in Rachel's pinwheels. At first, I can barely make out the words. I look at Ian, planning to say I like it. But he sits, teeth clenched like he's listening real hard. Finally, I catch the refrain:

Gliding up to the sky;
Driving, feeling so high!
Rachel, your grave's been dug.
Poor little Rachel, crushed like a bug!

And suddenly, I feel like someone's sitting on my lungs. I need to roll down the window, for air, or maybe to scream. But I can't make my hands work. I look at Ian, wanting to shake him, wanting to say, "It's not funny." But he stares ahead, blue eyes—Rachel's terrified eyes—

meeting the road with an intensity that says, "No, it's not funny," like maybe he's trying not to cry. I look away, staring out the window until the song fades out on the final "Poor little Rachel" and I can try to breathe again.

He doesn't know, I tell myself. He couldn't. But it doesn't really matter because I know.

The next song starts. I listen a minute. Two minutes.

Finally, I can't stand it. I say, "Did you know her? Rachel Eisenberg, I mean?"

"Yeah." He looks away. "Yeah, I knew her. She was my cousin."

That pretty much kills all possibility of conversation. I stare ahead, trying to keep smiling, trying not to look at this person I don't know but have somehow wounded anyway. How many people have I hurt? Ian's voice and his wild guitar wail in the background and, finally, I close my eyes and pretend to sleep.

But I don't sleep.

The day of the accident was Nicole's birthday, her seventeenth. Nicole had given herself a fake ID for a birthday present, so we were celebrating. After school we picked up a bottle of Absolut and a twelve-pack at this liquor store everyone knew that didn't check IDs too carefully. Then we drove to Nicole's house to drink it. Nicole's twin brother, Austin—who I was majorly crushing—was there with his friend Brett, Nicole's crush. So we were all drinking, and I guess I lost track of time because all of a sudden it was six o'clock.

"Omigod!" I said. "Is that clock right?"

"Last time I looked." Nicole giggled. She was smoking a joint Brett had given her. She offered me a hit.

I waved her off. "I have to go."

"Go," Nicole said.

"We took your car. You have to drive me." Even in my vodka-soaked haze, I was getting a little hysterical. How had I forgotten it was Wednesday, Grandma day? My parents didn't make too many rules, but one was engraved in granite: Thou Shalt Always Attend Wednesday Dinner. Mom and Dad always got off work early and picked up Grandma from her retirement village. If I wasn't home by six-thirty, I got grounded for the weekend. "Please."

"Oh, stop it, Sammy. I'm too wasted."

"You just don't want to leave." I was crying by then, trying to talk Austin and Brett into going with us so Nicole would drive me. And at 6:25, all of us were crammed into Nicole's white Prelude, flying down Old Cutler.

"We're not going to make it," I said. "I am so screwed."

"You're, like, two minutes late, Sam. Call them. Say you're stuck in traffic."

We were going against traffic, but it still might work. "Where's the phone?"

Nicole grabbed her cell phone and reached to give it to me in the back seat. That was when I saw her. The bicycle girl. Why had I noticed her, riding on the bike path, her dark ponytail flying behind her like a flag?

"Shit, Nikki, watch where you're going!" Austin yelled beside me. I looked to see our car drifting into the southbound lane. Nicole dropped the phone and grabbed the wheel, trying to swerve right, going too far, heading straight at the bicycle girl . . . and the ficus tree behind her. The girl's terror-filled eyes were the last thing I saw before everything went black.

I open my eyes. Ian's tape has finished playing. We must be on the turnpike because there's nothing on either side of the car but trees.

"Nice nap?" Ian says.

"Yeah." Did I nap? "Were you close? I mean, you and . . . ?"

"Rachel?" He reaches for the tape in the tape player. "Yeah. We're the same age. We *were* the same age. Neither of us had brothers or sisters, so we hung together. Rachel was supersmart, and I'm special-ed. Dyslexic. She used to help me with homework and stuff."

I nod, unable to speak.

"She wanted to be a special-ed teacher." He fumbles with the tape. "She'd have started at Florida State this year if that bitch hadn't killed her."

That bitch. He means Nicole, I tell myself. Nicole, who's in jail now, charged with manslaughter even though it was my fault. Since I wasn't arrested, my name wasn't even in the paper.

"I'm sorry," I say.

"Yeah, that's what everyone says."

I close my eyes again, but all I can see is Rachel's face.

I wake to the sound of a horn. The car behind us is honking furiously.

"What's wrong?" I say.

Ian shrugs. "Ignore it. A lot of people have issues with my car."

I'll bet.

But a moment later, the car pulls beside me. The driver's gesturing furiously at our rear tire. I roll down my window.

"Your tire's going flat!" she yells.

That's when the bumping starts. *Thump, thump, thump!*

"Shit!" Ian mutters.

Thump!

"Do you have a spare?"

Ian doesn't answer. He steps on the brakes, letting fly a stream of curse words.

Thump, thump, thump!

Ahead, I see a Gas, Food, Lodging sign for the next exit. "Can we make it?" I say.

Ian slows more and the distance between thumps expands.

"Might as well try."

About a hundred thumps later, we're at a gas station in the town of Stuart, and Ian's talking to a mechanic named Marv.

"Needs a new tire," Marv says. "You've got a nail in the sidewall."

"It's not in the sidewall." Ian points. "It just needs a patch."

"I'm not allowed to patch the sidewall," Marv says stubbornly.

"You mean, you're not allowed to patch when you can screw some kids for the price of a whole new tire."

"Maybe you should try somewhere else," Marv says.

That gets me out of the car. I look at the tire. It's mostly flat by now, and air's seeping out like a punctured pool float. No way can we make it to another gas station.

"Excuse me," I say.

Marv looks at me, and I put on an expression I used to use with Dad—the one that generally got me what I wanted. Until recently.

"I apologize for my brother," I say. "He's just upset because we're late for my grandpa's birthday."

"Your grandpa lives around here?"

I nod. "Right over on Palm." I point in the opposite direction of the turnpike. "Grandpa turns ninety today. We drove all the way from Miami for the party."

Marv moves closer, away from Ian. "Well, you're not getting back to Miami on that tire."

I pretend to examine the tire again. "Maybe if you patched it, we could stop by and get a new one tomorrow?" When Marv looks doubtful, I add, "And we need a fill-up too, right, Ian?"

Ian stares at me. "Sure."

Marv scratches his head. "Well, if you promise to come back tomorrow . . ."

"Oh, I promise." I reach into my purse and get Dad's MasterCard.

"Is there a pay phone here? I have to call Grandpa so he won't worry too much."

Marv takes the card and points. "Right over there, Miss."

Ian follows me to the phone, shaking his head. "What the hell was that?"

"It's called being charming."

"Or lying."

"Sure," I say, thinking about all the lies I'm telling just by not telling Ian about Rachel. "I'm a great liar."

"An admirable quality," Ian says. "How'd you know about Palm Street?"

"Every town in Florida has a Palm Street." We reach the pay phone. "If you'll excuse me, I have to call Grandpa."

When Ian walks away, I dial 1-800-COLLECT and call home.

Dad answers.

"What is it, Sam?" he says when he hears my voice.

"You have to come get me." I explain the whole situation with Ian being Rachel's cousin. "Please don't make me go."

"That's just something you'll have to deal with," Dad says.

"But . . ."

"I'm sorry, honey."

The line goes dead. When I call back a minute later, the recording tells me Dad didn't accept the charges.

It crosses my mind that maybe Dad set this up, me and Ian. He wouldn't do that. Would he?

I go into the ladies' room to cry.

Twenty minutes later, our car's gassed and ready. Marv hands me my credit-card slip to sign. "I'll see you kids tomorrow morning?" he says.

"Absolutely," I agree.

I try to picture Marv's face as we head back toward the turnpike.

"This was a mistake," Ian grumbles. "I should never have taken this stupid job."

I look at him, surprised. "So, why did you?"

Ian laughs. "In an ironic twist, it was Rachel's idea."

My throat tenses. "Rachel's?"

"Yeah—my famous deceased cousin. Around March, she came up with this bright idea. Apply to be camp counselors. 'We need to give something back,' she said. 'Help those less fortunate.' 'You mean, work my whole summer without air conditioning for six hundred dollars?' I asked her. 'No thanks.' But Rachel talked me into it. Said it would be our last time together before college this fall."

He shakes his head. "Didn't happen that way."

I shiver in the air conditioning.

"So," I say, realizing. "So where I'm sitting, it was supposed to be Rachel?"

"Basically. When she got killed, I thought about flaking on the job, but I couldn't do it. She wanted me to go." He shrugs. "Now, I'm not so sure."

"What do you mean?"

"I don't know. I checked my tires before we left. Maybe this flat was, like, a sign. Like, maybe I should just drop you at camp and head home. Get a job at Mickey-D's or something. Commune with the French fries where they understand me."

"But you said Rachel wanted you here."

"Yeah. But Rachel's dead."

Ian reaches over and lowers the air conditioner. The word *dead* hangs in the air.

Finally, Ian says, "Look, I'm sorry. I know it's bizarre. I know I talk about Rachel too much, but I'm going to stop now. You don't have to pretend to sleep anymore."

"I wasn't—"

"You were. It's just . . . you ever feel like it's all changed in a minute? Like, somehow, everything you know, everything you believe, everything you are is gone for good?"

"Yeah," I say. "Yeah, that's exactly . . ."

I stop. I was about to say that's exactly how I felt the moment I woke in the hospital and found out that Rachel was dead. Before that, I was a harmless screwup. After, I was a bad person. But I don't say it. Instead, I shift in my seat. Rachel's seat.

"Exactly what?" Ian says.

"Nothing. I just know what you mean."

True to his word, Ian stops talking about Rachel after that. But me, I see her every time I look at him. Now, there are fewer Mercedes and more pickup trucks on the road, and we pass towns with names like Yeehaw Junction and Howey in the Hills. I try to keep the conversation going by asking him questions. So I hear about his song writing ("It's really easy. The music sort of comes to me."), why he dresses like he does ("All fathers and sons have to clash about something, so I figure better my hair than something more important."), and what it's like, being dyslexic.

"Everyone assumes you're a retard, so you get to watch how stupid they act around you," Ian says.

"That doesn't bother you?" I say.

"I can't do anything about what people think. Besides, I like being different." He turns to me. "Why are you being so nice to me?"

I shrug. "You're interesting."

"Yeah, right," Ian says. But he sort of smiles for the first time since we met. "Your turn."

"My turn for what?"

"Be interesting. Talk. What's up with you and your dad?"

"Nothing . . . what do you mean?"

"Cut the crap. When he dropped you off, the tension was so thick you could have cut it with a chainsaw. What's with that?"

I look out the window. "It's no big deal. I just . . . I got into some trouble last month."

Tell him.

"Tell me about it," Ian says. "I told you all my shit."

Tell him. A voice somewhere in my head screams it over and over. *Tell him about Rachel.* I want to unburden myself, tell Ian and let him spit in my face or shove me out of his truck or kill me. Maybe I'd feel better. I couldn't feel any worse than I already do.

"Well . . . ," I say, and I realize from my shaking voice that I'm going to confess.

"Tell me, Sam." Ian's voice is surprisingly gentle.

That's when I see the flashing blue light in the rearview.

I look at Ian's speedometer. He's going seventy-two. The speed limit is seventy. The officer turns on his siren.

"Shit!" Ian says. But he pulls over and gets out his license.

The trooper wears a hat and marches up to the car in black boots.

"You know how fast you were going?" he says.

Ian looks at me. "About seventy?"

"Eighty-five." The officer enunciates the words like a prison sentence.

"What?" Ian starts to argue, then looks at me. I shrug. "Whatever you say, Officer."

The guy goes to write the ticket.

"What, no cute way out of that one?" Ian demands when we're back on the road. "You couldn't have taken off your shirt or something?"

I shake my head. "No way you were getting out of that one. Not in this car, not here."

"Shit," Ian says. "Shit, shit, shit!"

"It's just a ticket," I say.

"Yeah, well, my parents take careless driving a little more seriously than average—for obvious reasons."

I feel a pang. "Yeah, mine too." And I think of Rachel and know I can't tell him after all.

Ian looks at the yellow ticket, then shoves it up into

the sun visor. "It's another sign." Then he lapses into a silence that lasts another two hours.

After we merge onto I-75, it begins to rain. And when I say rain, I don't mean a light drizzle. I mean a flood like God set his shower massage on the high setting. People are driving with their emergency flashers on or even pulling over to wait out the downpour.

"Maybe we should stop," I say.

"No way. We already wasted time with the flat tire. I need to get there early enough so I can turn around and come back."

"How about stopping for food? We've been driving over six hours."

Then I realize what he said and I say, "Turn around?"

"I'm going back to Miami," Ian says. "I was wrong. I wasn't meant to come here."

"But you have to stay," I say.

"Why?"

I can't answer that. Part of it's because it would be easier if Ian left. But I need him to stay. If he leaves, it will just be one more thing I've destroyed.

When the rain lets up, Ian pulls off the Interstate, into a McDonald's parking lot. "Gotta bleed the lizard," he says. "You coming?"

At this point, I'm terrified that if I leave the car, he'll go home without me. But hunger and the pressure on my bladder convince me I have to get out. So I follow him in.

I barely notice the guys. There are three of them, with shaved-looking crewcuts. Rednecks. Big guys, in a pickup with a Confederate flag in the window. They stare at us.

"Scary," I say.

"You'll see a lot more of that around here."

We go inside. I rush into the bathroom to pee. When I come out, Ian's nowhere around. I finally see him, through the window. He's by the truck, looking at his watch. Tough shit, I'm hungry. I head for the counter and order a chicken sandwich value meal. In a burst of philanthropy, I order one for Ian too.

When I finish gathering my ketchups and napkins, Ian's still by the truck.

He's there with the three rednecks.

"Would you look at this?" one of them gestures at the truck. "Undertakers. That why you have on all these black clothes?"

"Where you from, boy? Around here, we leave long hair for the girls."

"Samantha." Ian looks relieved to see me. "Come on."

"You ain't going nowhere, boy." The biggest guy gives Ian a shove. I wince as Ian's head smashes the truck with a thud.

"Don't touch me." Ian's voice sounds calm. With his head, he indicates that I should get into the truck. That's the exact moment the big guy notices the Star of David, hanging around Ian's neck.

"Would you look at this?" the guy says. "We got ourselves a Jew-boy here."

I head around to my side of the truck and throw the McDonald's bags onto the floor. These guys are ignoring me, so far, but that can't last long. I shut my door as quietly as possible. Through the window, I see that the big guy has Ian's chain in his hands now.

"I said don't touch me," Ian says.

"What you gonna do about it, Jew-boy?"

I meet Ian's eyes through the window. Pure panic. Just like Rachel's that day. My own heart is beating so hard, I feel like it might burst out of my chest and blow through the windshield.

Then I notice Ian's keys sitting on the driver's seat.

I reach for them. The guys still don't notice me, concentrating on Ian. I slide across to his side, start the motor, then put the gear shift in reverse. Then I throw open the driver's-side door, knocking the big guy almost to the ground. "Come on!"

Ian shoves me aside and jumps in. One of the guys goes after him, but between us, we pull the door shut and lock it. Ian guns the motor and takes off, leaving the three guys eating dust. A few seconds later, we're back on our way.

"Shit." Ian's still out of breath.

"You think they'd follow us?"

"Nah—too much effort. They'll just wait for some other long-haired Jew-boy."

Still, I notice he checks the rearview three more times in the next five minutes. He takes the next exit, the exit for the camp. The town is even smaller than the one with the McDonald's. No fast-food places, no people. Ian opens the window and spits. I think there's blood in it. The wet air blows his hair away from his face and, for an instant, he looks so much like Rachel, my whole body aches from seeing him.

"Well, that's it," he says. "Three strikes, you're out."

"What do you mean?"

"The flat, the ticket, the attempted extermination by three guys without opposable thumbs." Ian's voice shakes. "Not to mention the rain."

Which is starting again. I look at Ian. His words are sarcastic, but his face looks like he's about to lose it. I touch his shoulder.

"Ian . . ."

He shakes me off. "I can't take this. I wasn't meant to be here in the first place. Rachel was. And I sure can't stay now."

"But you have to."

"No, I don't."

I force myself to look at him. "What about Rachel?"

"Rachel's dead!" He screams it. "Dead, dead, dead! She doesn't have any opinions on anything anymore!"

His words make my eyes sting. I feel this lump in my

throat, spreading all the way down to my stomach like I swallowed something solid and I have to wait until it passes. The rain drives down, and in the dark, it looks like we're drowning.

Finally, I say, "What about the kids?"

Ian wipes the back of his hand across his eyes like guys do when they're trying not to let you know they're crying. "What kids?" Then, "They won't care."

"They will," I say. "You have a lot to offer them."

"Yeah, like what?"

"Well . . ." I think about it. "For one thing, you're talented. You can write songs. I bet everyone will want you on their team for skit night."

Ian shrugs. "Big deal."

"It is a big deal. I can't do it." I still look at him. "And besides, these kids . . . they're coming from a different place than us. They're not overprivileged suburban kids." I remember Dad's words: *People less fortunate than you've been.* "These are the kids who get the toys we donate to the toy drives. And you . . ." Again, I can't find the right words.

"I what?"

"I don't know. Most guys wouldn't relate to that. They're all concerned about their image and being cool."

"And I'm not cool?" His voice has a trace of mockery in it.

I feel myself blush. "Sorry."

Ian shakes his head. "Don't be. That's exactly what Rachel said to talk me into this job in the first place."

"Yeah." I touch his shoulder again, and this time, he doesn't shrug my hand away. "Yeah, I'll bet it was. And she was right. Even I could learn some things from you I bet—about not going along with the crowd."

Ian pulls up to a sign that says Camp Seminole—Giving Kids a Chance. We were supposed to arrive around five-thirty. But what with the flat tire and everything, it's closer to seven, and dark in the shade of the slash pines. Ian stops the car. He takes the key out of the ignition and just stares at the sign a long time.

"Rachel was right," I say again. "Please stay."

At that moment, the rain stops. We sit there a moment, and suddenly, I feel like Rachel's actually there in the car. *I'm sorry,* I tell her. *I'm so sorry.*

Then, "Keep smiling."

"What?" Ian says. "What did you say?"

I didn't realize I'd said it aloud. I look at Ian. "I said, 'Keep smiling.' "

Ian stares back at me. "Rachel used to say that all the time. It was kind of a joke we had, because she said I never smiled. I wrote it on her memorial—the one on Old Cutler."

"On the tree?"

Ian nods. He looks at the water running over the window. Then he starts the car and drives through the gate.

"It wasn't supposed to be this way," he says.

"I know."

The road through camp is winding, with nothing on either side but trees and palmetto scrub. Ian drives real slow over the rocky road. Finally, we get to a log cabin that says Director's Office.

"Are you getting out?" I ask.

Ian nods. "You're right. I have to. I need to." He opens his door and starts for the back of the truck.

And I realize there's something I need to do too. I follow him around. The rain's still dripping off the trees, onto my hair, my face, and I say, "Wait! I have to tell you something."

He stops in the middle of removing my duffel, and he looks at me. And in that moment, he looks so much like Rachel that it all comes back. The drinking and the crash and that horrible moment when I realized that I was alive and she was dead. I'll never forget as long as I live.

A big drop hits my face, and I wipe my eyes. When I look back up, I don't see Rachel anymore. Now, I just see Ian, staring at me. And I know I can't tell him. Not now. Telling Ian will make *me* feel better, but it will probably make Ian get back in the truck and leave. I can't let him do that, no matter how much easier it would be for me if he did.

It's the sort of thing I'll have to learn to live with somehow.

So I say, "I'm glad you're staying."

Ian nods. "Yeah. You know, it's funny. All of a sudden, I'm glad I'm staying too."

He tosses me my duffel bag and heads for the director's office.

Me, I stand there a second, listening to the dripping rain, looking at the word UNDERTAKERS blazing on Ian's window. What will happen when Ian finds out? And he will find out.

I don't know what to do.

Ian turns back, smiling for the first time since we met. "Coming, Sam?"

"Yeah," I say. "Yeah."

ABOUT THE AUTHOR

Alex Flinn is a lawyer and the author of two hard-hitting novels for teenagers. In her highly praised first novel, *Breathing Underwater,* the main character, Nick, literally hits his girlfriend. Forced by a judge to attend counseling sessions and keep a journal, Nick examines his anger and comes to understand the effects of living with an abusive father.

Alex Flinn's second novel, *Breaking Point,* deals with peer pressure, bullying, and school violence in a private school where rich students make life miserable for poor newcomers. Paul is one of the lonely newcomers until Charlie, a school leader, invites Paul into his elite circle. But Paul soon realizes what that acceptance will cost him and how it will endanger the lives of other students.

"Keep Smiling," the author reports, was inspired by a real-life accident where a high school girl, roller-skating on a winding road near the author's home in Miami, Florida, was struck by a car driven by a drunk teenager and died. The driver was tried for manslaughter, but the passengers in her car were never identified publicly. Alex Flinn found herself taking a strong interest in the case. She wondered: Could the girls involved in the crash ever lead normal lives? Did they deserve to? Remembering her own teen years, she confesses: "Though I was never much of a drinker, I often sped down that same dangerous road to make my curfew. What if I'd hit someone?"

*How will a pillowcase, a search for balls on a golf course,
and a meteor shower change the fact that Mick has resented
his baby sister ever since she came into his family's life?*

August Lights

Kimberly Willis Holt

The summer of my seventeenth year, I won my first golf
tournament. After always coming in fifth or sixth place, I
thought I deserved a celebration, but my parents had separated at the beginning of the summer, and by August
they began divorce procedures. Our home went up for
sale, Mom went back into interior design, and I spent
more time with my little sister, Franny, than I ever had.

Before Franny came, every August Mom spread
the picnic blanket in our backyard. Then she, Dad, and
I lay on our backs and watched meteors glide toward the

horizon. No matter how crazy and busy our day had been, life slowed down that one special night.

We had a first-row view because one of the perks of living in the Texas Panhandle was no trees, just lots of sky. The first time we watched I asked, "What is it? A falling star?"

Dad had said, "Mick, you're looking at a Perseid meteor." Then he proceeded to explain all about Perseid meteor showers. I felt lucky and grown-up that he'd share such a thing with me, and I practiced saying it to myself until I could say it just like him.

One night when I was nine and at camp, our Cub Scout troop sat around the campfire, roasting marshmallows, when Rodney Segal pointed out some cosmic dust wafting through the sky. "Wow, look at that shooting star!"

"It's a Perseid meteor," I told him. "It's debris caused from a stream of particles zooming out from the sun. They collide with the earth's atmosphere. Then they burn up and make meteors."

Dad winked at me, grinning like I'd hit a home run. My chest puffed up with pride. But Rodney and the other guys stared back at me like I'd told them there was no Santa Claus.

Viewing the Perseid meteor showers became my family's August ritual until Mom left for China to pick up Franny. Mom always cried at those commercials for the Christian Children's Fund, which I guess was the reason we sponsored a boy from Uganda and a girl from Haiti.

When I was eleven she got a harebrained idea that our family of three needed one more person. She'd read an article about how China had an abundance of abandoned babies. I remember thinking, Why can't we just get a puppy? I wanted a dog more than anything in the world.

Mom and Dad had refused, since we lived on the golf course and weren't allowed to have a fence. "I don't need to be chasing down a mutt running after golfers," Dad had said when I asked for one for my birthday.

It was Mom's idea to live on the golf course. Dad didn't even golf. When we moved from our tiny house on the south side of town to the Tascosa Country Club neighborhood, I'd traded living next door to my best bud, Conner, for a view of the eighth hole.

The day we moved in, Mom and Dad had a huge fight over whether or not to replace our living-room couch. Dad said our old one looked just fine. Mom said it looked shabby in our new home.

Now two weeks had passed since Mom had filed for divorce, and she and I were spending the weekend gathering stuff for a garage sale. After we'd priced the last item, an eggbeater that I swore I'd never seen in my life, I said, "There it is, one family's junk, another family's treasure."

Mom sighed, looking over the garage. The old couch that she and Dad had argued about years ago stood among mountains of stuffed animals, framed prints, blenders, and tons of other crap.

"Why did we get all this stuff anyway?" she asked to

no one in particular. She shook her head. The lines around her eyes had grown deeper, and her face appeared pasty.

The last time I'd spent time working in the garage was when Mom went to China. Dad and I turned Mom's office into a nursery. We'd moved boxes of fabric samples and wallpaper books to the garage and painted the walls Pepto-Bismol pink.

Mom returned two weeks later with Franny. "Meet your sister," she said, holding out the bundle wrapped in a white blanket for me to see. Franny was bigger than I thought she'd be, not like Rodney's baby brother, who looked like a raisin with hair. "That's because Franny is eleven months old," Mom explained.

She smelled sweet, like soap. But she looked nothing like our blond, blue-eyed family. Her tiny dark eyes studied me like they knew every bad thing I'd done. And short black bristles covered her head. The orphanage shaved all the kids' heads to control lice.

Dad asked, "Mick, don't you want to hold her?" I shook my head and walked to my room.

"Give him time," I'd hear Mom say. "This is so new."

My dad took to Franny more than I'd hoped he would. Instead of working late, he started coming home by six. He'd hang up his blazer, loosen his tie, then head to the rocking chair with Franny. They rocked until dinnertime, Dad's long feet slapping the wood floor while he sang Elton John songs. Instead of hearing "Rock-a-Bye-Baby," Franny heard "Rocket Man."

I guess I'd hoped Dad would barely notice Franny and say, "How's that Scout project coming along, Mick?" At fourteen, he'd made Eagle, as had my grandfather. He had high hopes for me to follow in the family tradition. That's probably why he'd been my Scout leader since I was seven.

The rocking-chair lullabies didn't last long anyway. A few months later, Dad got promoted, and he went back to working late and weekends. At home, he often wore a rag tied around his head for the migraines he started getting almost nightly, especially after he looked at the bills. He claimed the pressure from the rag helped his pain.

Now the old rocking chair wore an orange sticker marked $18.00. "It will probably be the first thing sold," Mom said. "Baby stuff usually goes fast."

Mom was right. A pregnant lady and her nervous husband offered fifteen dollars. Mom smiled and said, "Sold!"

By 5:00, everything else had sold, too. It was like seeing our life drive away, piece by piece, in other people's cars and pickups. I hadn't seen so many people in our yard since Franny's second birthday party. Back then, I'd hidden behind a bush and eaten three pieces of the sweet chocolate cake while I watched our backyard circus. Some kids lined up to ride Poky, the pony, while Bungles, the clown, twisted balloons into poodles, and a tipsy magician pulled red and yellow scarves out of his hat. That party must have cost a fortune.

At the garage sale, I tried to make change for people,

but Franny pestered me constantly with questions. "Why does the wind blow more on the prairies than in the mountains?"

"It just does," I muttered, ticked because she was interrupting, but mostly because I really didn't know why.

"How does the meter man know how much electricity we've used?"

"He reads the meter."

"But how does he read the meter?"

Every question led to another. She read chapter books on the third-grade level while every other kindergartner checked out picture books.

"How *does* the meter man read the meter?" she said, louder.

"Franny, I can't answer you right now. Go play!"

When Franny was two, Mom had enrolled her in every class imaginable—ballet, tap, jazz, gymnastics. She even tried to put her in piano lessons, but the piano teacher said she didn't take students that young. Mom seemed to be on a campaign to prove that Franny was special. She hit the jackpot when at two and a half, Franny pointed to a can of chicken noodle soup, spelled out c-h-i-c-k-e-n, then announced, "chicken." I couldn't figure out when she'd learned to read. No one seemed to be coaching her. Mom enrolled her at St. Andrews but first insisted they test her. The IQ test results proved what even I'd suspected: Franny was a borderline genius.

The Monday after the garage sale, Mom had an

appointment with a potential client. "Watch Franny for me tonight, okay?"

"Okay," I said, though I'd planned to collect golf balls that evening. By dusk most golfers were on their last holes, and I'd be free to roam unnoticed on the eighth through the tenth. Most evenings I discovered five or six lost balls, but on a really great night I found as many as twenty. I never had to buy any balls and I made a nifty little profit from selling some to my teammates.

Before leaving, Mom said, "I really appreciate what a trouper you've been, helping out with Franny. I don't know what I'd do without you."

You better start planning, I wanted to say. I'd be off to University of Texas in a year. Austin was hundreds of miles away from Amarillo, hundreds of miles from the marital mess with my parents.

Until recently, I hadn't watched Franny since a few months after she arrived. Back then, Mom had asked me to watch her while she drove to the Toot 'n Totum for milk. I agreed, but when Franny cried, I ignored her, turning up the music on my CD player. Before I knew it, Mom stood in front of me with Franny in her arms. Franny's cheek pressed against Mom's shoulder, and her chest heaved as her cries wound down, becoming shallow. Mom flicked off my stereo and glared at me.

"Mick! This is irresponsible. Franny is your sister." The look of disgust on her face made me want to coil into a ball, but I just stared back.

For such a tiny human being, Franny had managed to make big changes in our family. Besides, I hardly ever saw Dad, and he and Mom began to fight about money all the time. Sometimes in the heat of their arguments, I'd secretly wished they'd never adopted Franny.

When Mom left for her appointment, Franny asked, "Are you going to walk on the golf course?"

"Nah, not tonight." I flicked on the TV.

"But you always go. Who will find the golf balls?"

"Don't worry about it. They'll be there tomorrow."

"I'll go with you."

"Read your book."

"I want to go," she said. "I can hold the pillowcase."

Punching the remote button, I did a quick run-through of each of the seventy-five channels. There was absolutely nothing worth watching. I looked over at Franny. She wore a black turtleneck, and her hair was pulled tight in a ponytail with a pink bow. The mountain of pillows on the couch practically buried her little body.

"Can't we go, Mick?"

"All right, come on. I guess you won't stop bugging me if we don't go."

She leapt off the couch, knocking several pillows to the floor. And like I'd seen Mom do a million times before, she plumped each one and returned it to its original spot.

"I'm ready," she said.

"Do you have to go to the bathroom?"

Franny shook her head. She was the reason that our car trips took so long. She had to pee every twenty minutes.

"Go to the bathroom anyway."

She sighed but obeyed.

I heard the water run a long time after she flushed. Like Dad, Franny washed her hands for two full minutes before every meal and after every flush, like it was a religion. Even at Boy Scout camp, Dad had used precious canteen water. If there had been a Boy Scout badge for immaculate hygiene, he'd have earned it.

Before leaving, I dashed upstairs and got a pillowcase from the linen closet. Franny and I headed out the back door and left our yard for the manicured greens.

"Why do you play golf?" Franny asked.

"Because I like it." That wasn't completely true. I learned to play golf because it was a sport Dad had never had any interest in learning and because it filled the space where Scout meetings had once been. When I quit Scouts that year, Dad had said, "I'd hoped you'd hang in there and make Eagle."

I knew he wanted that for me more than anything. He'd saved a place on his office wall for a future framed newspaper clipping of the three of us, Gramps, Dad, and me. The headline would read "Third Generation Eagle Scout." And even though Dad was disappointed in me, I felt pleasure in hurting him. After all, he'd resigned as my leader just so he could work more hours.

Almost immediately after stepping onto the greens, Franny found a ball. She squealed and ran for it. "Look. I got one!"

"No squealing," I told her. "You'll get us in trouble."

A few minutes later, she found her second one.

"I have two," she whispered, excited. "You have zero."

"This isn't a contest."

Her smile faded. She looked down at the grass. I wish I hadn't spoken harshly, but she was so competitive. Her dance trophies filled a shelf next to my lone golf one that I'd received for the tournament I'd won. She'd compared us then, too. "I have five trophies. You have one."

I tried to remind myself that she was only six and I was seventeen. We walked along not saying anything, while the trill of the cicadas stirred our quiet. The wind kicked up, and I got a good whiff of manure from the cattle-feed yard miles away to the south.

"Smells like money," Mom once had said. Dad had added, "Someone else's money."

A light turned on in a house. The family who lived there sat around their table, eating dinner. I thought back, trying to remember the last time we'd done that.

Franny had to walk fast to keep up with my long strides. I noticed for the first time that she walked just like Mom, her toes slightly pointed out like a duck. Though Franny's walk had a gracefulness that Mom's lacked, her legs moving effortlessly as if she were floating across the grass.

When I spotted a ball a few yards ahead, I decided to ignore it so that Franny could find it, an apology of sorts for snapping at her. But she surprised me and didn't pick up the ball. She saw it all right. I could see her little slits narrowing in on it. But she glanced up at me like she was waiting for me to retrieve it. I didn't, and we both walked past it. She glimpsed back, and I knew it must have killed her that she hadn't picked it up.

At the ninth hole, I told her, "If you check the outer edges near those backyards, you'll probably find a couple."

"Aren't you coming?"

"Go for it."

She hesitated.

"I'm going to the other side," I said. "I'll meet back up with you."

She glanced toward the yards, then at me. "It's just that it's . . . getting darker. There might be dogs."

Two years after Franny arrived, my parents almost gave in to letting me have a dog. I convinced them I would walk him three times a day and keep him on a leash when we went outside. Every day I checked the classifieds, searching for a Border collie or a golden retriever. Then Franny got bit by a neighbor's dog. Seven stitches later, no dog. I hadn't realized she was still afraid of them.

"Okay, I'll go with you. You really need to get over this dog thing, Franny. There are a lot of dogs in the world."

We made our way to the edge of the golf course that touched Bermuda grass.

"Have you read *Shiloh*?" she asked.

"The book about the dog and the boy?" I'd read it in fourth grade.

"Yes, and the mean man. I wouldn't be afraid of a dog like Shiloh."

"He's not real. He's in a book."

She grew quiet, squatting with her hands resting on her knees as she searched for golf balls. After a moment, she asked, "Do you think Daddy will come see us when Mommy divorces him?"

"Of course." Only I'd wondered that myself. Dad had hardly been around the last couple of years, just breezing in and out of our house to the office like a hotel guest. Ever since he'd moved out, he'd hardly spent any time with us.

"Why did you ask that anyway?"

"I don't know. He forgot to pick me up from dancing last week."

"He did? How did you get home?" I wondered why she hadn't called me. I had my license.

"My teacher called Mommy, and she came to get me. Mommy called Daddy from the car and yelled at him. She drove so fast, I thought she'd have an accident. She asked Daddy why he didn't want to be my father." Even though it was growing dark, I could see her chin quiver.

My gut ached. I'd heard similar arguments, but the way Franny said it made my parents' fights seem more real, more hurtful. "She shouldn't have said that. She's just ticked about the divorce."

"Then why is she divorcing him if she doesn't want one?"

"I don't know. They're adults. They don't always make sense."

She brushed her hand across the grass, then let her fingers crawl through the blades. "Do you think Daddy would stay with us if I looked like him?"

"What kind of crazy thing is that to ask?"

"You look like Mommy and Daddy. My friend Katy said she was special because she looked just like her daddy. He takes her to dance class every week. Sometimes he takes her swimming."

It dawned on me, for the first time, that Franny never knew the dad I knew. The dad who took me to Scouts, taught me to swim on Saturday mornings, played Nintendo. Franny only knew the dad who worked late at night and most weekends.

"Look, Franny, there are a lot of kids out there who don't look like their parents. That doesn't mean they're going to get divorced. It doesn't mean they won't either. It's not your fault that Mom and Dad screwed up their lives."

"But why don't *you* like me, Mick?"

Her words made my face sting. I swallowed hard. I wanted to tell her she was wrong, that I liked her, maybe even loved her. But I realized she was right. I'd chosen not to like her. Not because she didn't look like us, but because her arrival seemed to change so many things in our lives. I'd built a fence around her so high she couldn't possibly climb over it. And the funny thing was that now I knew Franny had nothing to do with the crumbling of our family.

"Don't be silly," I said. "Come on, let's go home. It's getting too dark."

We turned back toward the eighth hole. Silence overcame the night and I longed for Franny to ask one of her annoying questions, anything to bridge the river of quiet between us. *How do we know the world is round? Did George Washington really have wooden teeth? Do fireflies have tiny light bulbs on their butts?* But she asked nothing.

Part of me thought of saying, *Franny, you may not look like us, but you walk like Mom and you waste a ton of water, washing your hands just like Dad.* Instead, when we got to the spot where the ignored golf ball lay, I nudged her. "Hey, is that one?"

She raced up to the ball and picked it up. "Yep, you're right." She threw it in the sack, and we headed home.

"We only found three," she said.

"*You* found three. And three isn't bad. Better than zero."

Franny looked up at me, and I smiled, trying to reassure her that finding no golf balls wasn't a big deal. Her shoulders relaxed and she smiled back.

When we reached the porch, I took the pillowcase from her. "Wait here. I'll be back quick." And when her eyes widened, I added, "Promise."

Leaving the pillowcase on the kitchen table, I raced upstairs to the linen closet, grabbed the picnic blanket, and returned to the backyard. I spread the blanket on the ground, lay flat on my back, then patted the space next to me. Franny followed my example.

"What are we doing?" she asked.

"Just wait."

The moon, in its quarter phase, grinned down on us. I felt thankful that the sky was clear, and I fought back the sense of urgency that made my heart pound against my chest. A moment passed. Then I broke the silence.

"Dad used to rock you every night when you were a baby, Franny."

"He did?"

"Yep. Every night."

She smiled, and I wanted to stand up and cheer. But I didn't because right then a meteor slid across the sky, heading toward the horizon. I pointed in its direction.

Franny gasped and touched my arm. "What's that?"

And even though I knew her little brain with its big IQ could absorb the detailed explanation of the Perseid meteor shower, I longed to create some magic in her life. I took a deep breath and said, "It's a shooting star."

ABOUT THE AUTHOR

Kimberly Willis Holt grew up in a military family, living around the world, but her family's roots are in the piney woods of central Louisiana, the setting of her highly praised first novel, *My Louisiana Sky*. That novel was named an American Library Association Top Ten Book for Young Adults and a *Boston Globe–Horn Book* Honor Book, and won a Josette Frank Award, among other honors. Her third book, *When Zachary Beaver Came to Town*, also received numerous awards, including the National Book Award for Young People's Literature.

But short stories are her first love, she says. This one is set in the Texas Panhandle, where she now lives with her husband and daughter. The roots of her story go back several years, to the time when she met a writer who was going to adopt a baby girl from China. That woman's ten-year-old son was the same age as Kimberly Willis Holt's daughter, and she was curious about his feelings: would he resent a sibling after being an only child? A couple of years later when she met up with them again, the son was a thoughtful big brother who seemed proud of his sister's intelligence. "Still," she says, "I couldn't help but wonder, what if things had gone the other way?" She explores that alternative in "August Lights."

You can read more about Kimberly Willis Holt, including information about her most recent novel, *Dancing in Cadillac Light*, on her website: www.kimberlywillisholt.com.

❋

Seb doesn't get out much, and when he does one evening, he's surprised to meet a foreign girl who has no idea who he is.

The Kiss in the Carryon Bag

Richard Peck

Seb woke to find his feet were out of the covers, cooling. At the window, birds bickered. But the rest of the world—the rest of Europe, at least—seemed to be waiting.

He wasn't a morning person, even with a full night's sleep. He had a problem with that quick shift from dreams to the truth. Moments ago he'd been having his dream about the customized, stretched Range Rover. And where the back seat had been was a hot tub. And Seb himself was in the hot tub with a couple of—

Then gray morning.

He'd gone out last night. It was meant to feel spur-of-the-moment, but they'd planned. Things always had to be planned. Seb and Pauli and Rudy went out. Nothing special. Just out.

Pauli and Rudy came over and dressed at Seb's place, of course. Not Levi's and muscle shirts—a step up from that, cool but low-key. Rudy used to have a stud in his tongue. But it worked loose, and he'd swallowed it. Though he'd looked for it, he never found it.

So no metal on any of them. Pauli had brought Seb a pair of dark, wraparound glasses. They all worked a little bit on their hair. Then they went out. You could walk anywhere from Seb's place.

So then what? They thought about a movie, but they'd have to buck the line. They decided not to, not for Bruce Willis. Though it was early for a club, they swung past Airheads. The doorman, Paco, knew Pauli and never asked questions. They were in there if they wanted to be. But it meant bucking another line. They moved on.

They went here. They went there. Seb didn't even remember. He wasn't exactly cursed with total recall, as his old teachers used to say. And French grammar? Forget about it. Geography? Seb could barely find his way home.

They ended up at a new Internet café, just for a latte. You could see the whole place from the street—mostly glowing screens and a coffee bar where you picked up your own order. While Pauli and Rudy went to the counter, Seb sank into a deep armchair and scanned the

room. A few people online, a few more clustered around
little tables. No familiar faces—not that kind of place.

One minute he was gazing mindlessly around the
room. The next minute this girl was there, right by his
shoulder, looking down. Seb looked up. Everything began
to look up. She was on the border of beautiful. And very,
very close. Closer than any—

"I've just e-mailed everybody I ever knew," she said.
"Why send postcards, right? You get home before they do.
I don't even know where you buy stamps in this country."

". . . Ah," Seb said.

"You online a lot?" the girl asked.

". . . Not a lot," Seb said.

She had a fall of burnished red-brown hair. *Like
chestnuts by firelight,* thought Seb, who had become this
sudden poet.

"Oh. You're foreign," she said. "I mean, no, you're
not. *I'm* foreign, right? You live here."

"All my life," Seb said.

"I could tell," she said, "because of your accent."

"But you're the one with the accent," Seb said.

"No, I'm not," the girl said. "I'm from Indiana. We
don't have an accent. We just have a little bit of a twang.
You've got an accent."

He had to keep her talking. For one thing, she had a
wonderful accent. She had wonderful—

She glanced at the other two chairs. The one for
Pauli, the one for Rudy.

"I'm alone," Seb said. "Would you like to sit down?"

He started up out of the chair, but she put a hand on his shoulder. Then when she'd sat down across from him, he could still feel where her hand had been.

"Before I realized you were foreign—from here—I thought you might go to Park-Tudor," she said. "I figured you for private school. You know. Very blond. Probably tall. And you paid too much for the jacket."

Seb looked down himself. When he looked up again, the girl had leaned nearer. In a lower voice she said, "Personally, I'd ditch the shades. Wraparounds are so out. Especially after dark. Especially indoors."

She spoke like a spy. A lovely, lovely spy.

"Ah," Seb said. "I think I'll keep the glasses on."

"You're like the guys at my school," she said. "They probably wear their ball caps to bed. It's a security thing, right?"

". . . Right," Seb said. But now here came Pauli and Rudy, with the lattes. They saw her. Seb shook his head. They swerved to another table.

"I'm Aly, by the way," she said.

"I'm Seb."

"You're kidding."

"Sebastian, actually."

"Oh, that's too bad." For one perfect moment Seb thought she might reach out and touch his knee. "But then my real name is Alicia Mae. I was named for my grandmother."

"So was I," Seb breathed.

"You had a grandmother named Sebastian?" Aly's eyes were huge.

"No. I mean. It was my grandfather's. . . ."

But now she was smiling, grinning really. "You blush," she said. "It's like a sunset."

His face was hot. Strobing. From the other table, Pauli and Rudy watched like hawks.

Seb stirred, cracking a knee on the low table. "Would you like something?" he said. "A latte?"

He'd made it to his feet. He actually was tall, to his great relief.

"Whatever," she said, looking up at him.

"How do you like it? Your latte?" *Was that what you asked?* His head pounded.

"You decide," she said.

But Seb never decided things. He turned blindly in the room. Pauli and Rudy sat hunched at a table between him and the counter.

"She wants a latte," he whispered, dipping down to them, desperate.

"Is she an American girl?" Pauli muttered, watching her back.

"Yes."

"Better do as she says," Rudy said. "They expect that. Just go up to the counter and—"

"But I don't have any money," Seb said, low and hopeless. "You know that."

Pauli and Rudy had hardly touched their lattes. "Here, give me those." Seb swept them up. Careful not to spill a drop, he bore them away.

"That was quick." Aly looked up. She was all in black. Who wasn't? But on her it worked. "You ought to be a waiter. But that's the only tip you get."

Seb stared down, open-mouthed at everything about her.

"That was, like, a joke," she said. "Just sit down."

After the first sip, she said, "I think I've got you totally figured."

Doomed, Seb supposed.

"Correct me if I'm wrong," Aly said. "You're—what, seventeen, sort of?"

Seb nodded.

"Me, too, practically," she said. "I'll be a senior. And all the guys at my school are really, really immature, you know? But you—you're, like, younger than they are."

Seb sank back, relieved. Shattered.

"And I bet I know why." Aly lasered him with a look. "You go to an all-boys' school, am I right?"

Seb nodded. "I did. You saw right through me."

"Did? You've finished school?"

"School is finished with me." He didn't explain. He had his pride. "This place where you live, this Indiana," he said to change the subject. "How big a city is it?"

Now her eyes were enormous. "City? It's a whole

state. Like—the United *States,* okay? It's only about four times the size of this whole country of yours."

". . . Ah," Seb said. Aly had a white mustache now, from latte foam and double whipped cream, the way Rudy liked it. Chestnut hair, enormous eyes, white mustache. Seb felt faint.

She was telling him about this school "study tour" of Europe her class was on. They allowed three days for each country. The next stop was Norway, or Luxembourg, one of those.

"And you've enjoyed my country?" Seb strained to hit his stride.

"It's really small," Aly said. "Everybody in our group keeps bumping their heads. But it's nice." She dropped her voice and leaned nearer. "Though just between you and me, I'll never need to see another moat."

". . . Moat?" Seb began to drown in her eyes.

"Moat," Aly said. "You know. That wet area around castles."

Does she like me a little? he wondered.

"Are you seeing anybody?" she asked.

Through those glasses he was straining to see *her.*

"Like, are you going out with anybody? A girl?"

Seb couldn't get it together. Aly was wearing some kind of perfume, or something.

"Do you *know* any girls?"

". . . Not really," Seb said. "But there's this one girl.

Her family . . . my family . . . we've always known each
other."

"Oh, right," Aly said. "One of those deals. What's her
name?"

"Irmgard."

"Oh, that's too bad." Now she did reach out and touch
his knee. But then she checked her watch. "Listen, I've
got to get back to the dorm. Your buses stop running at
midnight."

"They do?"

Her eyes were huge again. "Hello. You don't get out
much, do you? You must have been in a boarding school.
This is the capital of the country, and it shuts down at
night like Kokomo."

"Oh," Seb said. She was on her feet now, dabbing off
her mustache. At their table Pauli and Rudy stirred.

Seb remembered to hold the door for her. After a
light rain, the cobblestones gleamed like little moons. A
historic building across the street leaned quaintly over the
pavement. "Shall I walk you to where the bus stops?"
Seb's hand and hers brushed.

"Do you *know* where the bus stops?"

". . . No."

Aly pointed the way. A few people were up on ladders,
draping streetlamps with flags in the national colors.

"Tomorrow's a holiday, right?" Aly said.

"Right," Seb said.

"There'll be a parade?" Her hand brushed his again.

Lightning struck in Seb's brain. *Was she hinting that maybe they could watch the parade together?* He panicked. "I can't," he blurted. "I'm . . . all tied up."

"Whatever," Aly said, and the bus loomed. Too soon, too soon. "And the next day we leave."

"For Norway," Seb said bleakly.

"Probably."

The bus doors wheezed open. She had one foot on the step when she looked back. "Tell me one last thing."

He'd tell her anything now.

"Do those other two guys follow you everywhere?"

The doors closed, and the bus lumbered away. Seb turned back to a large stone pillar. Behind it would be Pauli and Rudy.

But all that was last night. Aly had since morphed into being both girls in Seb's hot-tub dream. Now it was gray dawn. The birds were gone, but something stirred. A shuffling noise came from below the window, the sound of a lot of feet. Seb braced himself in the bed.

Then in an ear-splitting explosion, a full brass band struck up. The courtyard echoed and bellowed. The bass drum throbbed. Bagpipes whined. Cymbals crashed. It was deafening. The band had burst into "Happy Birthday to You."

The full choir of the National Cathedral erupted into song:

"HAPPY BIRTHDAY, QUEEN MOTHER, HAPPY
BIRTHDAY TO YOU!"

Seb grabbed his head.

It was a national holiday because this was the Queen
Mother's big birthday. She was a hundred years old today.
So of course it was a national holiday. But it wasn't a day
off for Seb. Because Seb was the Queen Mother's great-
grandson.

And heir to the throne.

II

Three rousing cheers rose from the courtyard to wish the
Queen Mother, rather unnecessarily, long life. As the last
cheer died away, Seb's bedroom door flung open.

They never knock, he thought. *They barge in like this is
public property.* Though being a palace, it probably was.

They were there in force today. In came the aged Head
Deputy Master of the Royal Household. "Your Royal
Highness," he said, giving Seb his first bow of the day.

Behind him came Seb's valet. After a quick bow, he
backed into the bathroom to draw Seb's bath. The barber
bowed in and backed to the bathroom after him. You
couldn't turn your back on royalty, so there were a lot of
people Seb had seen only from the front. Two footmen
brought in his breakfast, under silver covers.

Then a beat behind, Seb's lords-in-waiting—his
equerries—jostled each other through the door. They
were in double-breasted suits, and their shoes were pol-

ished to mirrors. But one equerry's necktie was practically around his ear. And the other one in his haste had buttoned up his suit jacket wrong. He seemed to list to starboard. They were Viscount Cricklemere and the Baron of Budleigh.

Pauli and Rudy.

His Royal Highness, the Prince Sebastian, sat in the carriage beside His Royal Highness, the Prince Reginald—Seb's little brother, Reggie. Seb and Reggie sat backward, across from the Queen Mother, who took up much of her seat. It was her personal state carriage, gold with cupids.

The parade got a late start. Seb and Reggie had been dressed, brushed down, and delivered on time. The King and Queen, their parents, already sat in their own personal carriage with roll-up windows so if they started in on one another, the public couldn't hear it. The King and Queen appeared together only on national holidays and postage stamps.

The Queen Mother herself had held up the show. She was just being hoisted up into the Cupid Carriage when the old dear remembered she'd forgotten her cough medicine. So stop the world. She went nowhere without it, carried it in a silver flask inside her giant handbag. She was deaf as a post but had a tongue in her head, and she wasn't going anywhere without her cough medicine. Footmen were sent.

Seb and Reggie could only sit there, smelling the horses. The Queen Mother looked suspiciously around under a hat the size of a satellite dish. Her mammoth handbag slid off her knees. Reggie reached down to get it for her, bur Great-granny was quicker. She snatched up the handbag and gave him a sharp clout across the ear with it.

"Yeow!" Reggie exclaimed.

"And you're supposed to be the smart one?" Seb remarked. "Even I know not to mess with her when her flask's missing."

It was said that while Seb would inherit the throne, Reggie had inherited the brains. Who from, Seb couldn't imagine. At ten, Reggie seemed nowhere near puberty, but he talked like a dictionary. He went to a special Swiss school for Gifted Royalty who were reading on grade level.

The day was warming up, and the horse smells were getting to be unbearable. "Why do we have to go through this?" Seb sulked. "I could be—"

"Because you are the Heir Apparent, Seb," Reggie explained in his high, annoying voice. "And I am the Heir Presumptive. We're the Heir and the Spare. When Daddy pops off, you'll be King, and I'll be—"

"Beheaded," Seb muttered.

The flask was handed up, and Great-granny's gloved claw grabbed it out of the air. Unscrewing the lid, she knocked back a shot, and the Cupid Carriage began to roll.

The parade ahead of them had been going on for some time. Every marching band in the kingdom marched. Then came the Royal Navy, with oars, and most of the army, on foot, displaying their only Hummer. Footballers marched in their shorts. The Royal Girl Guides pulled a float like a giant birthday cake with a hundred candles, unlit to prevent a firestorm.

After a drum and bugle corps passed by, the Cupid Carriage clattered out of the palace yard, behind plumed horses, toward the roaring crowds. Cameras flashed, and Great-granny snapped to, becoming the Queen Mother. Her gloved hand, rattling diamonds, came up, and she gave her roaring subjects her sweetest smile.

The breeze stirred the plumes on her stupendous hat. "Like a grenade going off in an ostrich farm," Seb muttered. Reggie was practicing his nod and his wave, like a little wind-up prince-doll. Seb slumped.

A heavy foot in a large high-heeled shoe shot out from under Great-granny's skirts and connected with Seb's ankle. "Give them a grin, you little git," she snapped, smiling in her modest way at the crowds.

So Seb had to pull himself together and play Prince.

He gave the crowds a small smile and a shoulder-level wave. When he ran a hand through his hair, several girls in school uniforms, perched on a wall, shrieked.

"Who *are* those silly girls?" Reggie looked around at him. "Could they have been cheering for you, Seb?"

"I wondered about that," Seb admitted modestly.

"They must be brain-dead," Reggie said.

With the hand that wasn't waving, Great-granny unscrewed the cap on her flask.

III

Cassandra Conway clung to the top of an ornamental fountain. Surrounded by spouting dolphins, the fountain stood in the capital's central square, the best place in town for watching the parade. Cassandra usually managed the best place for herself.

Clinging just below her was her more-or-less best friend, Aly Bidwell. The footballers of the Royal Playing Fields Alliance marching in their shorts had brightened Cassandra's day. But the parade was in a lull after them— large girls dragging a plastic birthday cake. Cassandra and Aly clung to the top of the fountain above a sea of fluttering, hand-held flags.

"Could you kill for a Big Mac with Special Sauce?" Cassandra said down to Aly. The capitals of Europe blazed with Golden Arches. But the American embassy had warned them against ground beef.

"Cass, get your boot off my shoulder," Aly said. They'd been dorm-mates on this trip through seven countries. Things were growing thin between them. At home, Cass had her own bathroom.

"Honestly, look at those dorky girls pulling that bogus birthday cake."

"Cass, shut up," Aly said. "We're not supposed to act like ugly Americans until we get home."

A drum and bugle corps passed endlessly by. Then behind feathery horses came a knockout of a solid-gold carriage, with cupids. Spoke wheels. Footmen with powdered wigs. The works.

"Here she comes," Cass cried, "the old woman!"

"I believe she's called the Queen Mother," Aly said.

"Whatever. Yikes, can you see her hat? It's like a giant auk. And who are those two with her? Are they, like, the princes?" Cass hung far out from the fountain. "Oh wow," she said. "Look at the big one!"

A well-timed sunbeam struck Seb's blond hair. He'd picked up the shy smile from Great-granny. He was perfecting her backhand wave. Cass nearly pitched off her pinnacle. "What are their names?" she yelled down to Aly.

"I don't know about the little one," Aly said. "But the big one's Seb."

"Seb?"

"I think I had a latte with him last night."

"In your dreams," Cass called down.

"No. For sure. He looks just like the guy I—"

"You wish, Jack," Cass replied.

By chance Seb's gaze swept the top of the fountain where two foreign girls clung, one on top of the other. The top one hung far out into space. It was the other one she was standing on who caught Seb's attention.

He lurched, and Reggie thought he might leap to his feet. Reggie's little hand closed over Seb's wrist. "Don't upstage Great-granny unless you want a thick ear," Reggie advised. Seb subsided.

But his eyes met hers. It was—

"Aly!" Seb called out, loud over the crowd, though Great-granny wouldn't hear.

"Hey, Seb!" Aly yelled back. "How about a latte?"

Cass swayed. Her parents had laid out three grand for this trip, and it was *Aly* who got to meet a prince? Cass felt like both the ugly stepsisters in *Cinderella*. She ground a boot heel into Aly's shoulder.

But Aly didn't feel a thing because as the gold carriage passed below, Seb blew her a kiss.

Seventy girls in the central square vicinity blew kisses back. But it was a kiss for Aly, and she knew it. She only nodded down to Seb, a little mock bow for his Royal Highness or whatever, and sent him a smile she hoped he'd keep in mind.

He was still looking back as the carriage went by.

And in her carryon bag of souvenirs, Aly tucked away a first kiss from a prince. True, he'd had to hurl it fifty feet. Cass said it didn't count.

Aly said, excuse me, but it did.

ABOUT THE AUTHOR

Everyone who knows Richard Peck—and by now everyone should—senses that he has as much fun putting his characters into interesting situations as readers have reading about them. No one who's read his famous short story "Priscilla and the Wimps," the Blossom Culp novels, or his two award-winning novels about Grandma Dowdel—*A Long Way from Chicago* and *A Year Down Yonder*—can forget those delightful characters and the hilarious situations they find themselves in. But Richard Peck is also no stranger to painful topics in his novels, having written about peer pressure *(Princess Ashley)*, rape *(Are You in the House Alone?)*, suicide *(Remembering the Good Times)*, and censorship *(The Last Safe Place on Earth)*. His novels have earned him just about every major award in the field, including the Newbery Award, an Edgar, the Empire State Award, numerous Best Books for Young Adults, the ALAN Award, and the Margaret A. Edwards Award for lifetime achievement.

What everyone may not know about Richard Peck is that he is something of a royal watcher. He says, "I like to see history still happening, and the more picturesque, the better." As a result, during one of his many visits to London, he was in the cheering crowd outside Clarence House in August 2000 "to see the Queen Mother of the English royal family roll forth in her glittering carriage to celebrate her one-hundredth birthday." Her great-grandson rode separately, he noted. And so he was inspired. In his story, he is quick to note, the prince, the principality, and the great-granny are strictly fictional.

※

Ricky's mother expects her rugged boyfriend, Dean,
to teach Ricky something about outdoor life,
but Ricky isn't sure he wants to go on this hunting trip
into the upland wilds of Hawaii.

Mosquito

Graham Salisbury

Ricky Gomes was sixteen but looked twelve.

Five-two, stretching it. Clear eyes and baby skin.

But all that was hidden now, as he stood waiting in the predawn shadows, holding the long rifle balanced at its midpoint. That's how he carried it, balanced in one hand, because it was almost four feet long, and when he stood it on end it made him feel short.

Beyond the grassy yard, a dark ocean nudged ghostly wavelets over the reef. It was a time Ricky liked, this early-morning stillness. He liked the time right after sunset, too, when he took his book out and read by the sea. It was the peace he wanted, the comfortable solitude.

"You ready, boy?" Dean said.

Dean was his mother's new boyfriend. Ricky didn't even know his last name, only that he was three years younger than his mom, hard-muscled, and tall.

Ricky shrugged. "Yeah."

Dean's dog, Moses, an impure black Lab, registered every movement Dean made, his ears cocked and ready.

Dean saw Ricky gaping and grinned.

Ricky didn't want to ride anywhere with the dog, and he especially didn't want to hunt with it. But Dean said that's what Moses was for. Dean should have called the dog Shredder, or Scorpion, Ricky thought. Moses didn't fit.

When Dean snapped his fingers, the dog bolted into the jeep and started pacing the back seat, whining low to get going.

"Get in," Dean said to Ricky, nodding toward the jeep. "He won't bite you."

Dean set his own rifle, a Winchester pack rifle, on the floor by the back seat, then slipped in behind the wheel. The engine coughed, caught, and fired up. Dean pumped the gas, revving it, then turned to Ricky.

Ricky climbed in with his rifle, an old .22 single-shot, bolt-action heavy piece he'd had for as long as he could remember. It used to be his dad's, and now Ricky had it because his dad had been lost at sea in a hurricane eleven years ago. Ricky'd never shot the rifle. Never had a reason to. Besides, it weighed twelve pounds and was hard to hold up.

But now Dean was taking him hunting.

Ricky's mom was more excited about it than Ricky was. She'd said, "You worry me, sometimes, you know that? You read too much. You sit around and look at the ocean, always going off in your head somewhere."

She studied him, frowning. And all he'd said was he didn't want to go hunting.

"There's a world around you," she said, almost pleading. "And you're missing it, Ricky. This is your chance to get out and see something new. Dean's a real outdoorsman. He'll help you learn things. Watch him. Ask him questions. He'd like that. Can't you just try it?"

And, finally, Ricky said, "Okay."

Now, with the dim headlights illuminating the way, Dean drove out onto the road and headed down along the coast toward the village. There, they would turn inland and head up the mountain, then park and hike even higher through the muddy guava zone to the big trees and pasturelands beyond. Wild pigs rooted around up there, Dean had said. Maybe some goats.

Dean drove without speaking.

Moses whined whenever they passed another dog at some shack along the snaky old road that climbed the island. Whined, but never barked.

The rifle lay heavy on Ricky's knees. He wondered how hard its kick would be, if it would knock him over when he shot it. He thought it probably wouldn't, not a .22. It wasn't powerful like Dean's lever-action 30-30, which Ricky had watched Dean fire. That one was loud, and its recoil could probably knock you clear to Honolulu.

"How come you go by 'Ricky'?" Dean said suddenly.

Ricky turned to look at him.

"How come you don't just say Rick? What are you, eleven, twelve?"

"Sixteen."

Dean glanced at him, raised his eyebrows. Then said, "'Ricky' is kind of sissy, ah? Like a girl's name."

Ricky didn't know what to say.

Dean's hair blew in the wind, short on the sides and long in the back. He was two years out of the army, and worked dry wall. And he had that dog.

They drove four miles uphill to Holualoa, and parked by the Chevron station where the road up met Mamalahoa, the road that circled the island. Dean shut the engine down, the dog whining louder now, knowing. Crashed cars sat rusting in weedy plots alongside the road. Kimura Store slept across the street. Nothing else but jungle.

They got out, each with his rifle.

Moses dropped soundlessly down and vanished into the weeds and trees, heading toward the uplands.

"Aren't you afraid he'll run away?" Ricky said.

"Nah, you just follow his bark."

"But he doesn't bark. He's kind of weird."

"He will when there's something to bark at. You'll see."

Ricky'd never hunted before. He'd been too young when his dad was around, and anyway, from what little he could remember, his dad hadn't been that much of a hunter. He liked to shoot at tin cans, though. Ricky'd watched that.

But Dean was different. He ate slimy raw *wana,* those venomous, spiky black sea urchins, fresh-picked from the reef. He buried cowrie shells in the sand and let the ants eat the meat out, then pulled them out stinking like rot to sell to tourists down at the pier. He carried a pair of forty-pound dumbbells in the back of his jeep, and pumped them in public when he was bored.

Ricky's mom thought Dean would be a great teacher, show Ricky all the man stuff she couldn't. "Look at him," she's said one time when he came over right after working out. "The man's a lean-mean-muscle-machine." Ricky looked at the muscles popping out on Dean's arms and chest. "Punch it," Dean told Ricky, pointing at the ribbed muscles defined in ridges across his gut. "Go on, you can't hurt me." Ricky nearly sprained his wrist. Dean's stomach was as hard as a sandbag.

They left the jeep and hiked up through someone's fenced property—jungle, and then a pasture. From there all the way to the top of the mountain, there were no roads and no people, nothing but the eerie, quiet highlands.

Ricky kept his gaze on four cows with heads turned toward them, gaping eyes, standing off a ways. It felt weird being in the same pasture with them. What if they charged?

He felt better when they climbed over a rock wall and followed a muddy animal trail into the dark and twisted guava zone that separated civilization from the clear, dry highlands farther up. He had to walk hunched down, pushing branches aside, letting them snap back behind him.

Ricky's arms blossomed with bloody red scratches, pushing through with the rifle already growing heavy in his hands. At least he'd worn his boots. He silently thanked his mom for that. He wasn't going to wear anything at all on his feet.

Dean stopped, suddenly alert. "Listen."

Moses seemed a mile away, the faint echo of his barking brushing the stillness.

Dean started running, slashing at the weeds and branches with the butt of his pack rifle, heading toward the barking. Ricky kept close, not wanting to lose sight of him. It would be easy to get separated, or maybe even lost.

When Moses fell silent, Dean slowed to a walk.

"Stick close to him, Ricky," Mom had said. "Learn something. The more skills you have the better off you'll be in this world. Go find out what you're made of."

Ricky wanted that, to prove himself, both to his mom and to Dean. Especially Dean.

An hour later they broke out of the guava into a knee-high wildgrass clearing. Trees and jungle on all sides.

"Watch out for cows," Dean said. "They're on the wild side up here."

Ricky checked in every direction, especially behind him, and often. What he didn't want was some wild thing sneaking up on him. He'd never been so alert in his life. It was a new world up there. It looked familiar, but it sure didn't feel that way.

They stopped to rest in the shade of a towering tree at the edge of the clearing. Dean leaned his 30-30 against the trunk. Ricky did the same, relieved to set his rifle down. It had gotten heavier and heavier. But soon he would shoot it. That would be good. He didn't drag it all that way for nothing.

"You any good at climbing trees?" Dean said.

Ricky looked up, squinting. "I guess," he said. "Yeah. Small ones."

"How about one like this?" Dean said, his hand on the trunk.

The tree seemed to go almost to the sun. How would you even get to the first branch?

Dean circled the trunk, looking for a way up. He

studied the lowest branch, eyeing it from one angle, then another. "I think we can do it, if I give you a hand up."

"But what for? I don't want to climb it," Ricky said.

"I need you to get a look at the land, see what's around us. I'd go myself if I thought I could get up there. Come, come, don't make me wait. Here, put your foot in my hand."

Ricky hesitated, looking up again, stepping back to get a better view. How far would he have to go? He didn't like high places. They made him dizzy. No, he wanted to stay on the ground.

Ricky stepped into Dean's cupped hands.

Dean lifted him to the branch with an ease that surprised Ricky. A smooth, clean toss, almost like a ride in an elevator. Ricky grabbed hold of the branch and struggled himself up onto it. After he'd found his tree legs, he stood and climbed one branch higher and waited, hugging the trunk.

"That's the way," Dean said, standing back. "Go a little bit more high and see if you see anything interesting."

"Like what?"

"Anything. Just tell me what you see and let me figure it out, ah?"

Ricky went higher. Then higher. Then stopped. It was as high as he wanted to go.

"What do you see?" Dean shouted from below.

"Nothing. Too many branches."

"Go up more, then. Or crawl out on that branch."

Ricky didn't move. He couldn't. His hands started to sweat and tremble. And his ears quivered with fear. "I . . . I can't. I'm . . . I . . ." His words trailed off until there was only the sound of the slow breeze rustling the leaves higher up.

"Hold on," Dean said.

Ricky glanced down, Dean now looking wobbly, like watching a car coming at you down a hot road. Swirling. Ricky blinked, but the dizziness only got worse.

Dean dragged a fallen branch over to the tree and made a ramp out of it, leaning it up against the trunk. Then he walked off a ways and sprinted back, running up the ramp and leaping to the low branch. He pulled himself up onto it.

In less than a minute Dean was just below Ricky, then above him, having gone around the other side of the trunk, and up. "Give me your hand," Dean said.

Ricky didn't move.

"You got to see this, Rick. Come on, give me your hand."

Ricky reached up. Dean pulled him higher. Ricky gripped the branch with steel fingers, settling next to Dean. Dean lifted his chin toward an opening in the leaves. Ricky gaped out at the purple-blue nub of the mountaintop far beyond. It was treeless up there, the land barren and foreign.

"Nice, ah?" Dean said.

"Yeah." It really was nice.

They were silent a moment. Ricky could feel the heat off Dean's body. Could smell his sweat.

"You ever wish you could fly?" Dean said.

Ricky shrugged, but Dean didn't see it, still gazing out at the mountain.

"I do," Dean went on. "Scare myself sometimes, because when I get up in a high place like this I just want to jump off and glide down . . . like a paper airplane, you know? I can almost feel it. You ever think like that?"

"No."

Dean leaned back and eyed Ricky.

Ricky glanced at him, then away. Dean was kind of strange.

"Shall we jump?" Dean said.

"What?"

"Us two. Jump and fly."

Ricky's eyes must have looked like they were popping out of his head. Dean laughed. "That's a joke, Rick. But you can still jump if you like. Me, I got pigs to hunt." He chuckled and shook his head, then started back down.

Leaving Ricky.

"How am I supposed to get down?" Ricky said.

"Same way you got up."

It took Ricky a good half-hour to lower himself to the first branch, then drop to the ground. He sat back on his heels in the dirt and tried to settle down, the fear still fluttering in his gut. He was never going to climb another tree in his life.

He looked up.

Nothing.

"Dean!"

Ricky stood, then noticed the 30-30 leaning up against the tree, right next to his.

"Boo!"

Ricky leaped and stumbled back and fell, a high-pitched scream escaping from some deep place inside him, a sound he'd not released before.

Dean laughed his head off.

Ricky wanted to yell at him for scaring him like that. "Are we going hunting or not?" he spat.

It was a brave thing to say. He usually didn't lash out, especially at adults. He was immediately sorry he'd done it.

But Dean was laughing.

Ricky stood and brushed himself off.

They grabbed up their rifles and headed north through the big highland trees, eucalyptus and pine.

A while later, Dean stopped suddenly, and crouched. Ricky dropped down beside him.

Dean put a finger to his lips, then pointed with his chin.

Two wild cows.

One dirty red, the other black and white.

"Stay low," Dean mouthed.

Ricky followed him, stealthing through the trees, circling around behind the cows. Closing in on them. Dean stopped and motioned for Ricky to squat and wait.

Ricky didn't like being that close. The cows were scrawny and rib-worn, and looked as if they would charge you if you got in their way.

Dean crept closer, coming up behind the dirty red one, hunching, stopping, squatting, waiting. Both cows grazed, unaware. Dean was good, Ricky thought. He could sneak up on anything.

Slowly, slowly, Dean crept closer.

The red cow never lifted its head.

But when Dean jumped up and lunged the last few feet and grabbed its tail, the red cow bellowed and rose up arching, kicking its legs back toward Dean.

Dean let go and fell to the grass, howling with laughter. The cow staggered and dipped, with its eyes about to roll out of its head. Then it thundered off, the black and white cow raising dust, going off in another direction.

Dean staggered up hooting after the fleeing cows, hands on his hips. He wiped his eyes with the back of a hand, his laugh slowing.

Ricky gaped.

"Bring my rifle," Dean called.

Ricky blinked, then went and got the two rifles and carried them out into the open field. Huh, Ricky thought. His .22 was almost twice as heavy as Dean's Winchester.

"Where's that dog?" Dean said, taking the 30-30 from Ricky.

Ricky looked back into the trees.

Dean whistled.

They waited.

"Ah, he'll find us," Dean said.

They hiked on, now walking parallel to the slope, neither gaining nor losing elevation. It felt stranger and stranger to Ricky, being way up in the highlands where there were no houses or people or anything he was used to having around him. Just the land. And the sweet smell, like dry grass after rain. And the eerie silence.

What was up here, anyway? Ricky wondered. Big Foot?

He gripped the rifle, glad he had it. Sort of.

The distance between Dean and Ricky grew, Dean not even looking back to see where Ricky was. What would happen, Ricky wondered, if he were to just sit down? How long would it take before Dean figured out he was alone? Would he come back?

Maybe not.

Ricky picked up the pace.

But it was hard, because he was thirsty and the rifle was heavier than a lead baseball bat. And why hadn't they brought canteens? Ricky'd just come along, trusting that Dean would take care of everything. You always took water when you hiked. Didn't you?

A while later Ricky heard Moses barking again. Dean started running, and so did Ricky, but Ricky lost sight of him in less than a minute.

There was no trail. Only a few places where Ricky

could spot flattened grass where Dean had run. Soon he lost even that. The heavy rifle slowed him down. And his throat was a hot, dusty wasteland.

"Dean!"

Ricky heard a shot.

He swung around and ran in that direction. The weight of the rifle was unbearable now, and awkward to carry while running. But he'd need it if he ran into a boar.

He stopped to listen, gulping air and sweating. Nothing at all now. Not even a bird or whisper of wind in the treetops.

Ricky crept ahead, hoping, praying, that he'd see Dean soon. A bead of sweat rolled down his cheek, the sun boiling in the open meadow. He didn't like being alone, not here.

He walked and walked.

Dean was nowhere.

Something rustled the weeds behind him.

Ricky gasped and whipped around. Moses stopped when Ricky stopped. The dog looked beat, his tongue flopping out, dripping with sweat.

"Hey boy, good boy," Ricky said, hoping he could cover the fear that raced through his body.

The dog growled, then suddenly stopped and looked up, ears cocked, as if he'd just caught some sound. He whined.

Ricky looked where the dog looked.

Moments later, Dean broke out into the open, heading toward them. "Where were you?" he said. "I thought you were right behind me."

"I . . . I got lost . . . but Moses found me."

"You hear the shot?"

"Yeah."

"Wild goat."

Ricky waited, wondering if there really were wild goats on the island. Ricky'd never heard of that before. Dean knelt to retie his boots. They had red stuff on them. Ricky wondered what that was.

The dog settled down in the grass, panting.

The heat.

The fire in Ricky's throat.

"We should have brought some water," Ricky said.

Dean glanced up. "Why?"

"Well . . . aren't you . . . thirsty?"

"Nope. Found a stream."

You drank from a stream?"

"Sure. Why not?"

"My mom said streams have parasites. The water could make you sick."

Dean finished tying his boot and stood, his 30-30 loose in the crook of his arm. "She ever been up here?"

"No."

"Then she don't know what she's talking about, huh?"

"I guess not."

"Anyway, what's going to pollute the water way up here?"

Ricky shrugged a shoulder. "I don't know. The cows?"

Dean shook his head. "Let's go."

They walked on, and this time Ricky worked harder at keeping up. More than anything, he wanted Dean to carry his rifle. He could barely hold it up any longer. It was too much, too heavy. What had his dad kept it for, anyway? He was a fisherman, not a hunter. Maybe he'd just liked the feel of it in his hands, like Ricky did himself. It was just too heavy, that's all.

"Where's the goat?" Ricky asked.

"Somewhere."

"Did you hit it?"

Dean didn't answer.

Moses moved on out ahead of them, but clearly visible. Not running off like before. Maybe he was getting tired of this, too.

"Yeah, I hit it," Dean said a while later.

"Huh?"

"Winged it. Stupid thing moved just as I got the shot off. I followed the blood for a while. But when I hit the stream I lost him."

They walked on.

Ricky said nothing, suddenly feeling kind of sick, because he knew that Dean was telling the truth. He could tell by the dark reddish stuff on his boots—that was blood. Ricky could see the wounded goat in his mind, trying to stay up, trying to get away, stumbling, staggering on, leaving blood all over the weeds Dean had walked through.

"Can you carry my rifle?" Ricky said, trying to get the goat out of his brain. "It's too heavy."

Dean stopped and turned back, half his mouth curled up in a grin. "You want me to carry both of them? Yours and mine?"

Ricky didn't answer.

Dean shook his head and continued on.

The stream was more like a small creek, barely six inches deep. And it wasn't really running. It dribbled down in places, but mostly it was a series of ponds with scum on top.

They stopped.

"Here's your drink," Dean said.

Ricky studied the water, then knelt at the edge of one of the ponds. Filmy on the surface, hazy-green and mossy below. Mosquitoes rose up and buzzed his head, sang in his ears. He jerked back, his hands flying around his face. The water was covered with larvae, or something like that. Every pond was a mosquito hotel.

Dean grinned. "Kind of dainty, ah, you?"

Ricky turned and looked off into the jungle.

"Don't move," Dean said.

Ricky froze. What?

It felt as if he'd been hit by a frying pan. Dean's slap shot from his cheek to his brain in flashing white stars, ringing in his ears.

"Mosquito," Dean said, showing Ricky his bloody palm.

Ricky touched his face, blinking back the water quickly swelling in his eyes.

Dean turned back toward the stream.

"Look," he said. "You drink like this. I show you how."

Ricky shook his head, trying to shake off the stars.

Dean got down on his hands and knees, and came up to the water like a dog. He brushed the watery film aside with the side of his hand, then blew on it for good measure. "See? A clear spot."

Ricky knelt, still slapping at the mosquitoes.

Dean drank. Ricky watched his throat gulping the water, and when he was done, Dean sat back and wiped his dripping chin with the shoulder of his shirt. "Minerals," he said, grinning.

Ricky bent close, blew on the surface. Moses settled in nearby and lapped up the filmy water.

Ricky moved away, up one pond. He brushed the scum aside like Dean had and tried to drink. But the green slime and blood-sucking mosquitoes made his stomach turn. He sat back. "That's okay. I'll wait till we get home."

Dean shrugged and started off, heading downstream, following the flow.

At one point, he stopped and crouched, motioning to Ricky like he had when he'd spotted the cows. Dean pointed through the tress to a clearing. A pheasant stood chest high in the weeds, looking up as if it had heard them.

Dean nudged Ricky to shoot it, grinning.

Ricky looked at the bird, like some feathered piece of art. Beautiful in the sunlight.

Dean elbowed Ricky again.

Ricky shouldered the rifle. He hoped he was holding it the right way, like Dean would do, because Dean was watching.

Ricky had to bolt a bullet into the chamber. He should have had it ready. And it was a regular bullet, when he should have had a spread shot, probably, for a bird. At least that's what he thought he should have.

The pheasant didn't fly off at the sound of the bolt when Ricky chambered the small brass bullet. Lifting and holding the rifle was like lifting and holding a sledge-hammer. Ricky could hardly keep it level.

He aimed, his hands weak and wobbly from carrying the rifle all day. He grit his teeth, not wanting to miss, not with Dean watching him the way he was. But the sights wouldn't stop wandering off the pheasant. Ricky held his breath. Easy, easy.

The bird has no idea he's about to die, Ricky thought. And that thought ruined it. Ricky didn't feel like killing anything.

Dean said, *Do* it! with his eyes.

Slowly, Ricky squeezed the trigger.

Click!

He pulled back the bolt and the bullet flipped out. Dean picked it up. Checked it over.

The pheasant fluttered off, rising away.

"Sweet Jesus," Dean said. "Lemme see that rifle."

Ricky handed him the .22.

Dean pulled back the bolt and squinted in. His hands were large enough to crush a cowbell. He laughed silently, his shoulders shaking. "It don't even have a firing pin," he said, tossing the rifle back.

Ricky caught it and looked into the open chamber to see for himself. But he had no idea where the firing pin was supposed to be. He made a disgusted look anyway, agreeing that, yes, there was no pin, and boy, didn't that just suck?

Dean, studying the dirt, sniffed and rubbed his nose. Then he stood and continued on down the streambed with Moses fanning through the trees on the other side.

What an idiot, Ricky thought of himself. What a fool. He could feel the heat of embarrassment crawling all over his face and neck. Stupid rifle didn't even work.

Ricky dragged himself and his rifle up and stumbled after Dean and the dog.

An hour later the stream meandered through somebody's pasture. They climbed over an old rock wall and started across it. Ricky spotted five cows and pointed them out.

Dean glanced that way, but said nothing.

There was a water trough at the other end of the pasture where a gate opened up into another paddock. A dull red salt lick sat smooth and half gone beside it.

But the water trough. Clear. No scuzz, no mosquitoes.

Dean unhitched the gate.

Ricky couldn't stand it. "Wait," he said. "I need a drink."

Dean turned back, his hand on the post.

Ricky leaned the rifle against the water trough and drank deeply from where the cows drank, not caring that there was grass in it, and what looked like cow spit or drool suspended below the surface.

The water was dark and clear and cold.

It slid down his throat, sweet and soothing. He could actually feel it go down through his chest. Like swallowing an ice cube.

Dean headed through the gate without looking back or closing it. Ricky wanted to drink more water, and even more, but he didn't want to get lost again. He grabbed up his rifle.

He stood holding it, looking at it. To carry it another step would break him. He knew it would, and anyhow he didn't care anymore. Who wanted a dumb rifle that was too heavy and didn't work?

He leaned it back up against the water trough. The guy who owned the cows could have it.

The lightness Ricky felt amazed him, the relief.

Just to walk.

Free.

Dean had gone on, leaving Ricky alone again. But there was the stream, and it flowed downhill. If he just followed that he'd eventually hit the road.

It took longer than he thought.

Dusk darkened the island, a cool shadow spreading down over the land, the trees, the jungles, and the serpentine road with no cars on it.

But Ricky was home.

The road was something he knew. It would take him back to the jeep and houses and people, downhill to the sea, to the rocks and his books.

Home.

He started walking.

"About time you showed up," Dean said from someplace Ricky could not see.

Ricky stopped and waited for Dean to show.

"Over here," Dean said. "In the ditch."

Ricky found him sitting in the long grass of a low spot alongside the road, trying to rub the goat blood off his boots with a handful of moist, green grass. He looked up and grinned. "Thought you might of got lost."

Ricky watched him rub at the red streaks. The grass wasn't working. It was just smearing it.

Ricky looked up. Beyond in the shade of an avocado tree, Moses lay panting lightly.

"Guess we got skunked, ah?" Dean said.

Ricky shrugged. "We saw some cows. And a pheasant. And you shot a goat, sort of."

"No, I didn't shoot a goat."

Ricky stared. "But you said . . ."

"I didn't shoot anything."

Ricky furled his forehead, thinking, What about the story? What about those bloody boots?

"Forget what I said. If anyone asks, we got skunked. That's all. Understand?"

Ricky didn't. "Sure," he said.

Dean threw the grass aside and dragged himself up.

They started down the road, the dog trotting at an angle ahead of them.

Nothing felt as good to Ricky as getting back to the jeep and sitting in it. And driving home, the engine heat coming down on his feet and legs like a hot bath.

They drove the whole way home in silence.

When his mom, standing out in the dark of the yard with them, heard about the missing firing pin, she laughed along with Dean, and Ricky watched them, wondering why neither of them had noticed that he no longer had the rifle with him.

"You're so silly, Ricky," she said. "No firing pin."

Dean spat and grinned.

"It's Rick," Ricky said.

"What?"

"My name is Rick, not Ricky."

"But honey, I like Ricky better."

Ricky turned and walked away, surprised, now, by the fact that he'd left the rifle up in the highlands and didn't even care. It was his dad's rifle. He should care about it. But he didn't.

He went into the house and got his book and a flashlight, now that the sun was gone. He walked out to the edge of the ocean and sat on the rocks, facing the sea. He read for a few minutes, then, when he couldn't concentrate, put the book down and turned the flashlight off.

He listened to the waves shushing quietly in, one slow roll after another. In the distance a lone boat light crawled along the dark horizon.

And the moon rose, glowing white over the mountain.

Two days later Dean dropped by in the late afternoon. Ricky was out in the yard with his mom, helping her trim back the bougainvillea. Dean drove down the dusty dirt drive with Moses sitting in the front seat like a human being, right where Ricky had sat.

Mom stood and thumbed a bead of sweat from her temple.

Dean parked and got out. "Stay," he said, and Moses settled down onto the seat.

Before coming over to the bougainvillea, Dean leaned over the back of the jeep and came up with a rifle.

Ricky's rifle.

He brought it over.

Dean *had* noticed he'd left it behind. Ricky caught himself holding his breath and gulped air. He'd never expected to see it again, and anyway he'd hoped he wouldn't. He didn't want it.

"Got her fixed for you," Dean said. "Firing pin and a sight adjustment. Was off a bit." He handed the rifle to Ricky.

"But I left—"

"Check the sight," Dean said. "Go on."

Ricky gaped at Dean.

Dean leaned over and kissed Ricky's mom on the top of her head, then put his arm around her. "Good time of day to work outside."

"That was nice of you, Dean," she said. "That gun was Ricky's dad's."

"Rifle."

"What?"

"That's a rifle, not a gun."

"Tst. You man, you."

Ricky held the rifle crossways. The stock had been rubbed with something. It was smoother than before. Kind of oily, now. And so were the metal, the barrel, and trigger guard. It smelled good, sweetlike.

"Got you these, too," Dean said, pulling a box of brand-new bullets out of his shorts pocket.

Ricky took the small box, surprised at its weight. He looked up, not knowing what to say.

Dean winked and dipped his chin at the same time. Behind him the sun sank, turning the shells of his ears pink and the halo of his head gold.

"It's a good one," he said. "You know what it is?"

"What what is?"

"It's kind of vintage, you might say. A Huntington & Richardson M12 Match Rifle. U.S. Army contracted them in the early eighties. Nice. You hang on to it, ah, Rick?"

Rick.

"I will," he said.

Later, out by the sea, Ricky sat with his book closed over a finger, marking his place. The rifle and box of bullets lay on the rocks next to him. Ricky followed the low swells moving in and watched, across the small cove, hundreds of black crabs scurrying around the mossy tide pools.

Watched and watched.

In a while, he set the book down and picked up the rifle.

Opened the box of brand-new bullets, took one out, and chambered it, bolting it in. Aimed down the newly adjusted sights at a large black crab. This time he managed to keep the sights steady.

He held the sights on the motionless crab.

Held, held.

Then squeezed the trigger.

The crab disintegrated.

For long minutes Ricky stared at the spot where the crab had been. His mind was blank, the reverberations of the fired rifle slowly dying in his hands.

A while later, he got up and picked his way across the rocks to the house. Loud music blasted out through the screened lanai door. Inside, his mother and Dean were laughing about something.

Ricky reached to slide open the door but stopped. His hand was trembling. He pulled it back and moved away, then slipped around the side of the house and climbed into his room through the window. He stood for a moment, not knowing what to do. The crab had just vanished.

Ricky eased down onto the edge of his bed in the darkening twilight. The sound of the endless sea shushed in, one slow wave after another.

"Rick," he whispered.

"I'm Rick."

* * *

ABOUT THE AUTHOR

Graham Salisbury grew up in the Hawaiian Islands, the setting of all of his short stories and award-winning novels. Among them are *Blue Skin of the Sea, Under the Blood-Red Sun,* and *Lord of the Deep.*

His many awards include the Oregon Book Award, the California Young Reader Medal, Hawaii's Nene Award, the Scott O'Dell Award for Historical Fiction, the Judy Lopez Memorial Award for Children's Literature, and the PEN/Norma Klein Award.

Many of his stories are based in reality, "Mosquito" being no exception. It is based on a very similar experience he had with his stepfather: carrying a heavy rifle that had no firing pin, drinking from a cow water trough, feeling small and uncertain about himself. He insists that his stepfather did pull the tail of a wild cow and drink from mosquito-infested waters. "What I wanted to do with this story," he says, "is suggest one of the ways a father might corrupt his son and dampen his sensitivity."

During his teen years, Graham Salisbury worked as a deckhand on a deep-sea charter fishing boat and was the skipper of a glass-bottom tourist boat. He later taught at an elementary school, was a graphic artist, and was a member of the classic rock band Millennium before becoming a full-time writer. He now lives in Portland, Oregon.

You can read more of Graham Salisbury's short stories about boys growing up in Hawaii in his newest book, *Island Boyz,* and find out more about the author on his website, www. grahamsalisbury.com.

❈

When Helene travels from Kansas to Cape Cod
to spend an adventurous summer with relatives,
she gets much more—and much less—than she expected.

Tourist Trapped

Ellen Wittlinger

Whenever I imagined spending the summer with my aunt and uncle on Cape Cod—and I imagined it often during the sixteen months it took me to save up the money to do it—I conveniently forgot to imagine my three-year-old cousin, Teddy, and the possibility that my relatives might be desperate for a live-in babysitter. I also hadn't imagined that by the time I got there, Lucy, my aunt, would be six months pregnant and under doctor's orders to lie around the house like a queen, making demands from a horizontal position.

For sixteen months I'd spent most of my Saturdays, not to mention holidays and all last summer, working at a women's clothing store called Lavender. Not at Abercrombie or Old Navy or some halfway decent store, because they were all at the mall in Groveland, which you needed a car to get to. In our family there were three cars and four drivers. As the youngest driver my mode of transportation was sneakers, and since Lavender was right in downtown Singleton, I could walk there. What luck!

Nobody under thirty shopped in Singleton, and nobody under seventy shopped at Lavender. I figured at least the store wouldn't be too busy and I could sit at the counter and read. Wrong. Even though the clothes are very expensive and incredibly ugly, the country club set loves them. They'll stand in line for cardigan sweaters with round, lacy collars, and cotton turtlenecks with ducks all over them. Or for dress-up, how about a chiffon sack with a huge gold belt which can be worn at the waist, or, if you prefer, buckled directly under your saggy boobs? Don't get me started on the underwear. The saddest part is that I'd get a twenty percent discount if there was a single thing in the store worth buying.

Sixteen months at minimum wage for helping Mrs. Humphries struggle in and out of every size-twenty slip in the store. For calling the ambulance when Alice Morse stumbled over the doorsill and sprained her ankle, twice. For smiling at that ancient Miss Callender, who brings back practically everything she buys, complaining loudly about the lack of quality workmanship these days, as if I made the clothes myself. Sixteen months of Lavender Ladies in exchange for six weeks on Cape Cod. What made me think that was a fair trade?

"Helene?" Lucy summoned me from her bedroom.

"What?" I yelled. I didn't feel like running upstairs every time she called.

"Do we have any more yogurt in the fridge?"

How did I know without looking? I put my book down to go check, then trudged upstairs with the report. "Nope. You must have finished it yesterday."

I could tell she was ready to burst into tears over this. Pregnancy had turned Lucy into a human waterfall. "Ooh, I really wanted some yogurt." Her mouth drooped at the corners and she cocked her head at me.

I knew what this meant—a trek to the country market half a mile from here. "Lucy, it's so *hot* out."

She sighed. "Believe me, I wish I could get out of this stupid bed and walk down to Dwyer's myself. I'm *dying* for some exercise."

And here I am throwing away the opportunity. "Couldn't I at least take your car? I've had my license for four months already."

"Wow, four whole months. Honey, you're not used to driving around here—the traffic is terrible in the summer. You could get lost."

"The store is right down the road—the village idiot wouldn't get lost!"

"Helene, you're my responsibility. I can't let anything happen to you, sweetie."

It seemed more like she was *my* responsibility. "What if Teddy gets dropped off before I get back?" He was enrolled in a toddler day camp with some of the neighborhood kids for a few hours every morning, and Lucy's friend Mimi, who also had a three-year-old, picked Teddy up and dropped him off for her.

"Don't worry about Teddy. He'll come and snuggle with me," she said. Which he would. He didn't like having his mother in bed all day, so he usually spent the first hour after camp curled up next to her, his fat thumb in his mouth. Then, when he got hungry and realized his mother wasn't going to get up today either, he'd track me down so I could make him a peanut-butter-and-honey sandwich—the stickiest meal possible—and then spend another fun-filled afternoon playing Candy Land or splashing in his plastic wading pool in the backyard. I'd been on Cape Cod for a week already and I'd seen the ocean once, from Jim's truck, during a storm. I might as well have stayed in Kansas.

"As long as you're going to the store, you might as well pick up another loaf of that bread Teddy likes, and get some tortilla chips and salsa too, for Jim." She smiled at me and winked. "What would we do without you?"

A good question.

Lucy and her husband, Jim, moved out of Kansas, where the rest of my family is stuck, about six years ago, right after they got married. Lucy is my mother's youngest sister, and she's always been what my mother calls *restless,* and my grandmother calls *a risk taker,* and I call adventurous. The rest of the family is perfectly content to stay within a fifty-mile radius of Singleton. The one vacation our family ever took, to Yellowstone Park, was fairly disastrous. Mom left her camera in a restaurant right after we took the picture which was supposed to grace our Christmas cards that year: my brother, Harry, and me pretending to push each other into Old Faithful—a historic moment, lost forever. Mom couldn't believe the camera wasn't still there when we went back for it, and she's believed ever since that everyone who doesn't live in Singleton is a thief. Then my dad had a fender-bender as we crawled through Yellowstone behind a line of campers and SUVs, and even though it was our headlight that broke, the other guy called Dad a retard, so my dad thinks that everyone who doesn't live in Singleton is "foul-mouthed." Hence, we do not travel.

Lucy was the one person in our family who enjoyed going places. She went to college in Arizona, where she met Jim. After school they spent six months or so wandering around Europe, and then Jim got a teaching job in Wellfleet on Cape Cod. Lucy e-mailed me the details: Cape Cod was a long, sandy peninsula, basically a big beach. They lived in an old house near a marsh and watched egrets and great blue herons—some kind of large birds—from their living room window. Lucy worked at an art gallery where she met all kinds of eccentric people.

It sounded like the *opposite* of my boring Kansas existence. Even when I was younger I'd imagine Lucy and Jim, and the beaches, and the birds, and the artists, and I'd think, *that's the kind of life I'm going to have someday!* I guess Lucy was kind of a role model or something. So when she wrote a few years ago and asked me to come for a visit, I knew I'd have to find a way to get there somehow. "We'll hang out at the beach," she wrote. "On the Cape you can wear your swimming suit all day long!"

When I was thirteen the never-changing-clothes angle was quite appealing, but by the time I'd saved enough money to actually get there, I was more excited about all the suntanned guys who'd be hanging out on those beaches with me. Of course now Lucy had become a beached whale, and I couldn't even get near the water because I was babysitter, grocery shopper, nurse's aide, and part-time cook for an entire family.

Before I got here, before she was sent to bed, Lucy had promised me picnics on the beach, trail walks in the dunes, art gallery tours, and theater trips. Now the plans had been rather drastically scaled back. Lucy said Jim would take Teddy and me to the beach on the weekend, but I could already see that scenario: Jim, fast asleep on a blanket, and me letting Teddy bury me in sand up to my neck. I might as well let him bury me completely—what would be the difference?

I got all the stuff Lucy wanted at the market, plus a bag of cookies and a *Spin* magazine for myself, and packed it into my backpack for the walk up the road. I was in no hurry to get back, since Teddy would have returned by now and would be waiting for me to hang out with him again. The thing is, I'm not one of those girls who just adore babies or are crazy about little kids. I gave up baby-sitting two years ago because I hate the way kids boss you around and refuse to do the stuff their parents said they would, like eat dinner and go to bed. I don't even know why people want to *have* kids—for years they're just whiny, sticky little brats. I tried to like Teddy, since he was my cousin and all, but I decided I could always like him later on, when he spoke English better and knew how to take a shower.

A bicycle pulled up alongside me and a girl jumped off it. "Hey!" she said.

"Hi." I wondered if she thought I was somebody else.

"I saw you going into the library a few days ago, with Mr. McCrory, didn't I?"

I nodded. "Yeah, Jim's my uncle. Do you know him?"

"He's your *uncle*? He was my freshman biology teacher. He's such a doll! Are you staying with them for the summer?" She walked her bike next to me.

"Yeah, for six weeks or so. I'm Helene."

"I'm Poppy." She brushed her hair back off her forehead to reveal two rings in her eyebrow that matched the one in her nose. "Do you have a bike?"

I shook my head. "No. I thought they'd let me drive one of their cars, since my aunt is kind of laid-up anyway, but they're being very paranoid."

"You can drive? Oh, God, you're so lucky. I have another year until I can get a license. You mind if I walk along with you? What's wrong with your aunt? I never met her. What's her name? Is she pretty?"

Poppy was one of those girls who sort of ran right over you. You weren't sure if she was actually speaking to you or just liked to hear her own voice. Still, she was the first person near my age I'd met since I got here, and the way things were going, she might be the last.

"Her name is Lucy, and, yes, she's pretty. Although she doesn't look so great these days. She's pregnant and she has to lie around in bed or on the couch all day, so she doesn't usually bother to fix her hair or change out of her pajamas."

Poppy made a face. "Gross! Poor Mr. McCrory!"

I had to laugh—poor Mr. McCrory didn't seem like anybody I knew. "Jim's too busy to mind. He's working for a carpenter most days and helping me take care of their three-year-old the rest of the time."

"Oh yeah, Teddy. I saw him once. He's the most adorable little boy, isn't he? God, I hope I have a kid that cute someday."

She babbled on, asking me a million questions about Lucy and Jim, until I started to feel like it wasn't any of her business. I knew kids liked to gossip about their teachers anyway, and I figured I'd already given her plenty of head-line news, so I got quiet.

Finally she said, "Listen, if they ever let you have the car, give me a call—Poppy Malone—and I'll show you around to all the cool places on the Cape."

"Thanks," I said. "That would be great."

She shrugged. "My boyfriend's on vacation for a whole month, and my best friend is grounded. I'm bored to death." She remounted her 3-speed and pedaled off down a side road. "Tell Mr. McCrory I said hi!"

That night at dinner—which was takeout pizza served on the living room coffee table so Lucy could lie on the couch while she ate—I told Jim about meeting Poppy. His eyes rolled back in his head.

"Poppy Malone! Of all the people you could meet!"

"Is that the one who was always stopping by to chat after school last year?" Lucy asked. "Who drove you crazy?"

"That's her."

Lucy laughed. "Sounds like she's got a big old crush on you, Mr. McCrory."

"That's what I thought too," I said.

"Oh, please. Don't say it." Jim sank back into the couch.

Teddy grinned and ran up to his father, throwing himself against Jim's knees and rubbing his tomatoey mouth on his pants. "I cwush you, Daddy! I cwush you!"

Jim roared with laughter and gave Teddy a big hug.
Lucy purred at the kid, "Oh, you old smarty, you! Give
Mommy a crush too!" She sat up and pulled Teddy onto
the couch with her.

"Be careful, Luce. You shouldn't lift him," Jim said.

"I'm careful. I have to hug my baby, don't I?" She
smothered Teddy with kisses and then blew on his stomach, which made him giggle hysterically. This is what I
don't get about parenting—do people really think every
little thing their kid says and does is so brilliant, or do
you have to lie to the kid all the time? I also can't imagine
wanting to do all that hugging and kissing with someone
who wears a diaper and smears jelly in his hair.

"So, would you rather I didn't see her anymore?" I
asked Jim, when the hilarity had died down.

"Oh, Poppy's harmless. I don't care if you want to
hang around with her."

"Helene," Lucy said, "you've been such a huge help
around here, *anything* you do is fine with us."

I decided the time was right to try again. "While
we're on the subject of things that are fine with you,
couldn't I please use the car once in a while?"

Jim looked at Lucy. "What do you think?"

"Jim, it's dangerous! Helene doesn't know her way
around here, and the traffic . . ."

"We have traffic in Kansas too! If I can't drive, I'll
never get to see anything!"

Lucy and Jim exchanged glances; I knew they felt bad

about asking me to help out around the house so much. I was appealing to their guilt.

"She could drive to the beach, couldn't she?" Jim asked Lucy.

Lucy, who'd hitchhiked in Italy and backpacked in Budapest, frowned. "It scares me," she said. God. Having kids was turning her into a complete wuss.

"We'll talk it over tonight," Jim promised me.

But that was the night everything began to change, and the last thing Jim and Lucy were thinking about was me. Lucy woke up at about three o'clock having contractions, the hard pains you have when the baby is ready to be born. Jim called her doctor and then he woke me.

"Helene, I'm taking Lucy to the hospital. Don't worry—she'll be okay. If I'm not back by seven o'clock, would you get Teddy up and get him ready for day camp? Just tell him Mommy and Daddy went to see the doctor—he knows we do that sometimes. He'll be fine."

"What's happening? Is the baby okay?"

Jim hesitated. "I hope so. I'll call you as soon as I know anything."

Of course I couldn't go back to sleep after that. I kept thinking about how Lucy already called the baby Maxie. They knew it was a girl and Maxine was the name they'd picked out. I thought about the times—just that night for one—that Lucy had picked up Teddy, even though she wasn't supposed to, because she couldn't stand not doing it. I thought about how she'd already spent a month lying in bed and was willing to spend three more like it, just to have this baby. It wouldn't be fair for her to lose it now.

Jim wasn't back by seven so I got up and got dressed before I went into Teddy's room. He was already awake, sitting up in bed and looking at a picture book.

"Hi, Teddy!" I said, all cheerful and phony. "Time to get up and have breakfast."

"Hi, Hewene," he said. "Mommy comin'?"

I sat down on his bed. "Well, your mommy had to go see her doctor very early this morning, and your daddy drove her there. They'll be back soon."

He looked at me, hard. "I want Mommy."

Yeah, and I wanna go to the beach, but it isn't gonna happen for either one of us anytime soon. "You know what? Your mommy said she wants you to get ready to go to day camp this morning. And I bet by the time you get home, she'll be back too."

Teddy put his book down. "You make me Cheerios wif drawberries?"

"No problem."

He followed me to the kitchen and downed his cereal in silence, although he kept glancing up at me, as though for clues. The kid obviously knew something was up—kids have radar. I kept chewing away on my own Cheerios, pretending to be having the breakfast of my life. Yum, yum, yum.

"I guess we better get you dressed," I said, as though nothing would be more fun. "Mimi will be here in twenty minutes."

Teddy's tiny bare feet followed mine back to his bedroom. I picked out a pair of red shorts and a striped navy blue shirt. Teddy only wore a diaper at night now, just for safety's sake, and he stripped it off by himself and tossed it aside. "Dwy," he said.

Which reminded me— "Maybe you should go to the bathroom before you get dressed."

He gave me that searching look again. "Okay," he said, and walked down the hall.

"Do you need me to help you?" I called, and was relieved when the answer came back no. I collapsed on the bed, exhausted already, but sprang back up when Teddy reappeared.

I helped him into his underwear, then the shorts and shirt, buckled on his baby sandals. "Mommy does my hair," he reminded me, so I found a soft brush and tried to slick down the fine, flying strands, without much luck.

He followed me out to the living room to wait for Mimi. Instead of sitting on the floor with his toys as usual, Teddy sat next to me on the couch, closer than I was used to. I smiled and patted his shoulder. He shuddered and began to cry.

"What's wrong?" I said, my voice still all fake happy.

"Don't wanna go 'way," he said, sobbing. "Wanna stay here and wait for Mommy!"

Now what was I supposed to do? I looked out the window to see if Mimi had miraculously appeared—she was a mother, she'd know how to handle this. But no, I was all alone with a terrified child. I sighed and kneeled down on the floor in front of him so I could see his face.

"Teddy, you don't have to cry. Mommy is coming home soon."

The look he gave me this time made me shiver. It was a look of pure terror, the kind of look an adult might have if you told him an atom bomb was due to land on his home in five minutes. Panic, horror. His world had *collapsed.*

Before I realized what I was doing, I had my arms around him—there was no other choice under the circumstances. He put his arms around my neck and wailed. I picked him up and walked up and down the living room with him. "Oh, Teddy, don't be worried. Everything is okay. Stop crying now. Your mommy is coming home soon." But he wasn't buying my line. He sobbed until we were both soaking wet.

Then Mimi appeared. I tried to give her the shorthand version of what was going on, without scaring Teddy even more. She seemed to understand, and when she reached out her arms to Teddy, the little traitor went right to her without a backward glance.

"He'll get you all wet," I warned, picking my blouse away from my shoulder.

"Teddy!" she said, ignoring me. "You know what stops tears? I do. And I bet your mama has some in the freezer."

Her voice was so authoritative. She obviously knew her way around toddlers. Sure enough, Lucy kept Popsicles in the freezer, which Mimi must have known. "A Popsicle will freeze those tears right up!" she said, grabbing a hand towel and mopping his face. "And then you'll be able to go tide-pooling this morning with all the other kids. Oh, we have to find your bucket and shovel and get some sunscreen on you, don't we?" Mimi had me running around looking for his baseball cap and beach towel while she described to Teddy all the fun things that were planned for the morning. She whisked him out to the car while his sobs diminished and the Popsicle ran down his arm. She even remembered to bring out a second Popsicle for her own kid.

How do people *do* this day after day, I wondered as I watched her car pull away from the curb. I was a wreck after one hour.

And just then the phone rang. Jim.

"Did you get Teddy off this morning?" he asked, sounding very tired.

"Yeah. He was a little upset—he wanted to see Lucy—but Mimi gave him a Popsicle and he was okay."

"That's good."

"So what happened? How's Lucy?" I almost didn't want to know.

Jim sighed. "Lucy . . . she lost the baby."

I was speechless.

"They couldn't stop the contractions and it was born . . . not alive."

"Oh, no! No!"

"The doctor said it happens like this sometimes. It doesn't mean she couldn't carry another baby to term. Just not this one."

"But she wanted this one so much."

"Yeah."

"Is Lucy . . . okay?"

"Physically, yes. But she's sedated at the moment. She was so upset . . ." Jim's voice broke then and I had the feeling he was crying too. "She really wanted a little girl. She really wanted . . . Maxie."

I didn't know what you were supposed to say when something like this happened. I felt sorry for them because they were obviously really sad, but I couldn't actually feel it myself. It wasn't as if a real person had died, was it? Just the idea of a person. I hung up the phone and went back to bed for the rest of the morning.

Lucy stayed in the hospital two days. Jim took Teddy and me along the day he brought her home. Teddy was so excited he dashed into the hospital elevator and punched all the buttons before Jim could stop him, so it took us a while to get to Lucy on the fourth floor.

She was already dressed when we got to her room. She smiled at us all, and Teddy leaped up onto her lap.

"Ooh," she cried.

"Teddy, you have to be careful," Jim said. "Mommy has been sick."

"No, it's okay," Lucy said. "I want to hold him. I want to hold him." Then she burst into tears and hugged Teddy so hard it kind of scared him. After a minute he pushed her away and struggled to get down. Jim picked him up.

By the time we got home Lucy was quiet. So quiet, in fact, that it was eerie. Jim asked her if she wanted him to order Chinese takeout and she just shrugged her shoulders.

"Crab rangoons? How about ginger chicken?" he asked.

She just nodded and walked into the living room. I followed her because it just didn't seem like we ought to leave her alone yet.

"Does it feel strange to walk around again?" I asked her.

"Everything feels strange," she said. "The whole house feels strange." She stood at the French doors and stared out into the backyard.

"Should I set the table outside? The breeze is cool."

Lucy gave me a long look, as if she was trying to remember why I was there. Finally she said, "Anything you want, Helene. It really doesn't matter to me."

And that was the way it was. Nothing *did* matter to her anymore. Jim and I were still the ones tending to Teddy, even though Lucy could get up now and walk around and do things. She didn't *want* to do anything.

I took over getting Teddy up in the mornings and feeding him his breakfast so Lucy could sleep in, but usually she wasn't asleep anyway. She'd ask me to bring her a cup of coffee, and then she'd sit up in bed, drinking that oily black stuff and staring at the sheets or the ceiling. Mimi and some of her other friends came over to visit, and left looking sad and confused. Nobody knew what to say to make it better. Or maybe there just wasn't anything *to* say.

It was hard on me, and harder on Jim, and hardest on Teddy. Some days Lucy wanted him to sit with her so she could squeeze him into pulp, and other days, when he *wanted* attention, she ignored him and just stared out the window at those stupid birds. Teddy got crankier and crankier by the day, and one morning, at breakfast, when I reminded him the day camp was taking a boat ride that morning, he slowly tipped his cereal bowl. By the time I realized what he was doing, there were Rice Krispies swimming in milk all across the table.

"Teddy!" I ran for a sponge. "Why did you do that?"

"Not going," he said.

"You're not going where?"

"Boat. Not going."

"It's the same boat you went on two weeks ago and

you loved it that time." I sloshed the cereal mess back into his bowl so I could dump it down the disposal.

"No, I didn."

"You *said* you did."

He shook his head. "Don't wike you, Hewene." He stuck out his little chin and wrinkled his nose to show me just how much he didn't *wike* me.

I could feel my face heating up. "Well, that's just tough, isn't it?"

It was the first time I'd let my real feelings out in front of Teddy. Forget the mature act—I didn't have the patience for it anymore. I'd already *been* patient for sixteen months of old ladies and their ugly clothes; I didn't go through *that* so I could go through *this*. I knew it wasn't fair that Lucy lost the baby, but it wasn't fair that I was losing my vacation either. After all, she could have *another* baby, although why she even wanted one was beyond me. I, on the other hand, could not afford another vacation.

I got Teddy's stuff ready without speaking to him. He sat silently at the table. Thank God he was already dressed. When Mimi showed up, I threw his bag over my shoulder, picked him up, which I seldom did, and marched out to the car.

Teddy screamed. "I thaid *no!*" He banged his fists on my arm.

"I don't care. You're going."

Mimi looked startled, but she didn't ask questions. All

I told her was, "We're having a slight meltdown around here."

"I'm not surprised," she said as she helped me buckle the squirming, screaming child into her back seat. I put his bag on the front passenger seat.

"I'm sorry you have to deal with this," I told her.

"I'm used to it," she said. "You should go somewhere this morning—get out of the house. Just because Lucy's not ready yet, it shouldn't stop you."

As I walked back inside, I decided she was right. If I waited around for permission to leave, I'd spend the entire six weeks waiting on these people. I got out the phone book and looked up Poppy Malone.

I felt odd calling somebody I barely knew, but under the circumstances, she was practically my best friend. She answered.

"Hi. This is Helene Walters. I met you the other day? You know my uncle, Jim McCrory?"

"Oh yeah! Hi! Did you get the car?" She sounded excited by the possibility.

"Well, no, not yet. But I thought if you weren't doing anything, we could take a walk or something."

"Oh, a walk?" She was disappointed. "I guess so. Where do you want to go?"

"I don't care. The only things I've seen since I've been here are the supermarket and the library. I'll go anywhere."

I called upstairs to Lucy that I was taking a walk. At

first it didn't seem to register with her, but just as I was going out the door, she yelled, "Be careful, Helene! Please!"

A few minutes later I met Poppy at the fork in the road where I'd left her a couple of days before. She had her hair braided in about twenty little braids, so you could see all the holes in her ears and eyebrows and other facial parts.

"There's a pretty good bay beach we could walk to from here," she said. "It'll take a while though."

"I guess I should be back by noon," I said, "although it's not like they're going to *fire* me if I'm late." Immediately I launched into the story of the miscarriage, and Lucy's stupor, and Teddy's anger, and my own impatience with the whole situation. I guess I really needed somebody to talk to who could understand my point of view.

"Oh, I feel so sorry for Mr. McCrory!" Poppy said, completely missing the whole point.

"*He's* okay. He gets up and goes to work every morning just like he always did. It's the rest of us who are going nuts."

"I'll bet he feels awful though. The way he talks about Teddy, you can tell he really loves having children."

When I didn't respond to this, Poppy considered my position too. "Of course, I can see where it's a huge bummer for you. Being on vacation and all."

"Right." Now she was getting it.

"If you can just talk them into letting you drive the car, we could go up Cape and go shopping or something. Orleans or Hyannis."

Shopping wasn't high on my list of vacation plans. "We could go to the National Seashore, couldn't we? I've never even been to any of the big outer beaches."

She shrugged. "I guess. It's kind of a tourist thing to do."

"Well, I'm a *tourist!*"

"Maybe we could get Mr. . . . *Jim* to drive us there someday."

"Jim?"

"Well, you call him Jim."

"He's my uncle."

"Could you *be* luckier?"

It was pretty obvious, by the time we got to the bay beach, that Poppy Malone was absolutely gone on my uncle. He was her favorite topic of conversation, plus, as we walked by three separate boys, she compared them, both favorably and unfavorably, to Jim. He was her standard of excellence. It was starting to creep me out.

The beach, however, was lovely, with soft white sand and little birds hobbling around by the tide line. "What are those pretty birds?" I asked Poppy.

"Those? Just sandpipers. They're all over." She lay back in the sand. "How old is Jim anyway?"

Enough. "Look, Poppy, he's too old for you. Besides which, he already has a wife and child, both of whom he loves. I think you should look for somebody else."

"I'm just having fun. I have a boyfriend, you know. That doesn't mean I can't enjoy looking around."

"Well, look, but don't touch."

She stared at me. "Kind of straight-laced out there in Kansas, huh?"

On the walk back, Poppy tried to make up with me. "You know, once you get a car, your summer could really turn around. There are some great concert venues up Cape—we could have a good time. And we can go to the beaches too. Wherever you want to go!"

"Okay, I'll keep trying, but I can't promise anything."

"Or, if you want me to, I could come over sometimes and help you with Teddy."

It would definitely make the time go faster to have Poppy around, and she would probably throw herself zealously into the job. But I was pretty sure it wasn't a good idea. The atmosphere was weird enough without Poppy there lusting after Jim.

Poppy and I went on walks every couple of days. We weren't much alike and I suspected neither of us would choose the other as a companion if we actually had a choice, but we didn't, and I really needed to get away from the house when I could. I was getting more and more resentful of my job as Teddy's surrogate mother. Lucy wasn't getting out of bed any more often now than she had when she was pregnant. Maybe less. And even when she was up, she was more like a ghost than an actual person.

And the more Lucy withdrew, the angrier Teddy became. Jim suddenly seemed to have more work than ever and Teddy threw a fit every time his father left the house. To tell you the truth, I felt like throwing a fit myself. All promises of days at the beach were forgotten. At some point I realized I had two weeks of my "vacation" left and I hadn't seen a damn thing that you couldn't walk to in under an hour.

That Saturday morning Lucy floated into the kitchen silently and sat at the table drinking her usual coffee while I made pancakes for Teddy. At least my homemaking skills had improved over the past month.

"Do you want some?" I asked Lucy.

"No, thanks," she whispered.

Jim came rushing through and stopped to pour the rest of the coffeepot into his thermos.

"Where are you going?" I asked.

"I told the guys I'd work with them today. Wanna get that place on Holden Road finished up." He looked at me. "Oh, I guess we could have gone to the beach today, but . . ." He grimaced and glanced at Lucy.

"Too hot at the beach," she said, sipping from her steaming cup.

I turned back to the pancakes. The room was silent. Jim sat on a chair to pull on his work boots. The pancakes were done, so I piled them on a plate and took them to the table. Teddy immediately pulled one off the stack and onto his plate, then started complaining, "I said booberries in mine!"

"We don't have any . . ." I started to explain.

"I hate you Hewene!" he yelled. "I said *booberries!*"

Jim looked up. "Didn't you get any blueberries at the store yesterday?"

For a minute I stood looking down at the stack of warm, fluffy pancakes. I thought I was trying to calm myself down, but I guess I was just getting ready to explode.

Jim started to speak again, something about how he'd made a list for me, blah, blah, blah, but he stopped talking when the first pancake smacked him in the forehead. The second one would have clipped his ear, but he caught it in his left hand. "What . . . ?"

Teddy shrieked with delight, picked up *his* pancake, and tried to sail it across the table at Jim too, but it fell short and knocked over Lucy's half-empty coffee cup instead. She jumped, moving faster than she had in weeks, trying to mop up the spill with her napkin.

I had two pancakes left, one for Teddy and one for his mother. Teddy thought we were in the middle of a great game and didn't mind at all being pelted with dough, but Lucy, who got it in the cheek, was so startled she almost looked awake.

A number of possible remarks passed through my head, but the only thing that came out was "Make your own damn breakfasts!" And then I ran upstairs to my room and banged the door. I was sick to death of being their servant.

Jim was the first person through the closed door.

"Helene, I realize this trip hasn't been what you expected, and you've been a good sport about it, but you have to understand . . ."

"I *do* understand. I've been understanding for a month now, and I'm tired of it. I worked for sixteen months to afford this trip and I haven't gone *anywhere*. All I've seen is the wading pool in the backyard!"

"I know that, and I'm sorry. Look, next weekend . . ."

"Oh, right, *next* weekend. I believe that."

By then Lucy had swept silently into the room with Teddy clinging to her leg.

"Helene," she said. "What do you expect of us? We didn't plan for this to happen while you were visiting. We didn't plan any of it!" The tears began to run down her cheeks. "Don't you think we would change it if we could?"

My anger turned to rage. "I know a terrible thing happened to you! I know it! But what would you do if I wasn't here? You'd get a babysitter, or a cook, or Jim wouldn't work so much, or *something*." Then, I couldn't help it, I started to cry, too. "I'm sick of being in this house all the time! I want to go home!"

Lucy was hysterical—she leaned into Jim as she yelled back at me. "You think *I'm* not sick of this house? Leave then! Go home! Get out of here!"

"I will!"

"Wait a minute, you two," Jim began, but then he didn't seem to know what else to say.

Teddy looked back and forth between his mother and me, his face crumbling, once again panicked by what he couldn't understand. I sank onto my bed, sobbing into my hands, and Teddy crawled up onto my lap.

"Hewene, don't go home! Stay wif me!" His fat little hands beat against my shoulders to make his point. When I looked at him, his lip started to quiver. "I eat my pancake, Hewene. It's good!"

I hated to see him looking so scared again and I put my arms around him. "You're a good boy, Teddy. It's not your fault," I told him. He plastered his chubby body against mine, hanging his head over my shoulder and grabbing me around the neck as if he'd never let go. The weight of him felt good, this small but very important person who needed me, who wanted me to stay.

Jim eased Lucy over toward the bed and they both sat down too. "Listen, we're all emotionally fragile right now. I realize we've been dumping too much onto you, Helene. You were doing it so well, I guess we started taking it for granted. I'm sorry. You're right, if you weren't here, we'd have had to deal with these things right away."

Lucy was still crying buckets. "I don't really want you to leave, Helene. None of us do. Don't go home!" She reached over and grabbed my arm.

"I don't really want to go home. I just want . . . a vacation!"

"Listen," Jim said. "I'm not going to work today. We're all going to stop crying and clean ourselves up. I'll go get blueberries and make a new batch of pancakes, as long as you promise not to hurl them at me. While we eat, we're going to make plans for the next two weeks, so that you don't leave Cape Cod without seeing it."

So that's what we did. Teddy kept holding on to me all through breakfast, sitting on my lap and eating his pancakes greedily. Lucy sat up straight and entered into the conversation. She was still sad, but she was making an effort now. When Teddy left my lap and climbed onto hers, she welcomed him eagerly and they cuddled like old times.

The most amazing thing that happened was Jim and I convinced Lucy to let me drive her car.

"It's such a risk, Jim," she said at first. "Haven't we had enough bad luck lately?"

"But Lucy," I said. "Everything is a risk. Walking, and driving, and flying here in the airplane. Getting married . . . having a baby. Just because it's a risk doesn't mean you shouldn't do it."

She sighed deeply. "I suppose you're right."

"Helene isn't reckless," Jim said. "I don't see a problem with letting her drive your car for the next few weeks."

Lucy nodded and smiled at me. "Sometimes I look at

you, Helene, and I remember the way I used to be, before I started to worry about everything. I like the reminder."

Jim told the carpenter he was working for that he was taking three-day weekends for a while so he could show his niece around, and Lucy started getting up in the morning and taking care of Teddy herself.

The first day I got the car, I called Poppy Malone and we made a plan to spend the whole day at Cahoon Hollow Beach and then have dinner and go to a movie. An entire day spent without speaking to a three-year-old!

The beach was beautiful and there were, indeed, several lifeguards on duty whose biceps were bigger around than my neck. I was happy just to watch them walk up and down the beach, but Poppy actually flirted with one of them, and then got annoyed when he didn't flirt back.

"Thank God Will comes back next week," she kept saying. "He is *so* cool."

It seemed like her interest in Jim was finally fading too. Apparently she'd "run into" him at the drugstore and he'd looked awfully seedy in his workman's clothes. Not like the spiffy sweaters he wore to teach school. "He just didn't seem like who I thought he was," she told me. I didn't argue.

We had an okay time. Poppy talks too much, and she probably thinks I don't talk enough. The movie was good, and I wanted to talk about that on the drive home, but Poppy wasn't much for discussing film theory. Mostly she wanted to sigh over Matt Damon.

I decided, now that I had the car, I could probably have just as much fun without Poppy along. She'd have her Will back soon anyway. The funny thing was I really wanted to take Teddy with me to the beach, to watch him play with the waves and make a sandcastle and generally enjoy the lovely place he lived. Lucy, of course, was worried about everything from my driving, to freak undertows, to being struck by lightning. I assured her I would not let a thing happen to the most precious person in her world.

The more time I spent with Teddy, the more I understood how you can feel that way about a child. All of a sudden, the sticky fingers and the stinky hair and all of that doesn't matter so much. You start *liking* it when they pick your lap to sit on.

One afternoon when Teddy and I were building a big fort at the beach, he stopped what he was doing and started giggling.

"'Member when you frowed that pancake at Daddy?" he said. "And you frowed one at me too?"

"Yeah, that was a pretty crazy morning, wasn't it?"

"Yeah. But you didn' go home, did you, Hewene?"

"Nope. I decided to stay with you."

"Yeah, cuz I wuv you da best," he said matter-of-factly as he lay on his stomach in the sand.

I stuck my arm down through the tunnel on my side until I connected to the tunnel on Teddy's side. Then I grabbed his wiggly fingers. "Yeah, I love you the best too."

ABOUT THE AUTHOR

A former children's librarian, Ellen Wittlinger attained prominence in the field of books for teenagers with *Hard Love* when it was named a Michael L. Printz Honor Book in 2000, as well as a Lambda Literary Award winner and an American Library Association Best Book for Young Adults. It's the story of a lonely boy and a feisty girl who calls herself a Puerto Rican Cuban Yankee Lesbian who meet through their interest in zines. Another interesting relationship between a lonely boy and an oddball girl— this one works at the town dump—develops in Wittlinger's more recent *Razzle*. Her other novels include *Noticing Paradise, Lombardo's Law, What's in a Name,* and *Gracie's Girl.*

Ellen Wittlinger lives with her husband in Swampscott, Massachusetts, across the bay from Cape Cod where "Tourist Trapped" is set. Her story is based on her own experience when, at sixteen, she spent the summer with her aunt and uncle in Los Angeles. Expecting to have a magical time, hanging out at the beach and meeting surfer dudes, she instead had to handle much of the housework and take care of her three-year-old cousin after her aunt suffered a miscarriage. She insists she did not throw pancakes but says she wishes she had, because she returned home "feeling used and abused (and not at all amused)." But, she adds, "None of my relatives were actually as annoying as THESE folks—that's why it's called fiction."

Ellen Wittlinger's newest novel is *The Long Night of Leo and Bree.*

✳

A recipient of the ALAN Award for Outstanding Contributions to Young Adult Literature, Donald R. Gallo is the editor of a number of short story anthologies for teens, including the highly regarded *On the Fringe, Time Capsule,* and *No Easy Answers.* The American Library Association includes his *Sixteen* among the 100 Best Books for Young Adults published between 1966 and 1999. A former junior high school teacher and a university professor of English, he currently spends his time as an editor, author, and workshop presenter, and interviewer of notable authors.

ACKNOWLEDGMENTS

A special thank you to Bill Mollineaux, C. J. Bott, and Ms. Bott's tenth- and twelfth-grade students at Shaker Heights High School for helping us choose a title for this book.